OiNK

OiNK

A FOOD FOR THOUGHT MYSTERY

J. L. NEWTON

SHE WRITES PRESS

Published 2017
Printed in the United States of America
Print ISBN: 978-1-63152-212-3
E-ISBN: 978-1-63152-213-0
Library of Congress Control Number: 2016959503

For information, address:
She Writes Press
1563 Solano Ave #546
Berkeley, CA 94707

Cover design © Julie Metz, Ltd./metzdesign.com
Formatting by Kiran Spees

She Writes Press is a division of SparkPoint Studio, LLC.

This is a work of fiction. Names, characters, places, and incidents either are the product of the author's imagination or are used fictitiously. Any resemblance to actual persons, living or dead, is entirely coincidental.

To "Polly" and Bill
and to the women and men of "Haven Hall"

Chapter 1
Monday, October 11, 1999

I'd dressed carefully that morning for the coffee date I'd agreed to in the afternoon—a silky dark green skirt, a thin white blouse, and malachite earrings, which gave my eyes a greenish cast. It was important about the eyes because my hair, as usual, hung straight to the middle of my neck. It had pretended to obey the curling iron at home, then slyly unfurled itself as soon as I stepped outside. I'd been divorced for a year, and though I'd dated several men, I hadn't yet found another to share my life. My daughter, Polly, lived at the heart of my existence, but I missed the third component of a family—not Solomon, God knows, my cantankerous and cheating ex-husband—but someone to take the role that he had filled, a partner for myself. Ten days ago, I'd placed a personal ad in the *Valley Bee* describing myself as "an academic, early forties, bright and good looking, the mother of a ten-year-old daughter, and the owner of a large, marginally trained dog." What I had not disclosed was that my field of work was women's studies. That often put men off and could wait until potential suitors met me.

I'd received several responses, one from a man with a teenage son. "Talk about the marginally trained," he'd written. But, uneasy about meeting men I'd never seen, the only letter I'd answered was from a colleague at my university—Wilmer Crane, professor of mathematics. I'd never dated a mathematician before, preferring men whose work I could actually understand, but a colleague, even in math, attracted me. As a member of my own community, he seemed familiar and somehow safe.

I enjoyed my solitary walk down Lupine Avenue and the pleasing views it gave me of the lawns and pathways between the gray stone buildings of the university. Taking a bite of the corn and cherry scone I'd bought for breakfast—it was part of my new research on food to make and sample recipes involving corn—I watched a gray fat squirrel dart after an even fatter one up the trunk of an acacia. Finches chattered in high tweeting sounds, two skipper butterflies fluttered orange and brown above the lawn, and the air, already warm against my skin, smelled pleasantly of newly mown grass. I was fond of this campus, which had the well-earned reputation of being an easygoing place, where people were smart but not pretentious. Perhaps a legacy of its agricultural college past—when students had come to study plants and pigs and cows—Arbor State had struck me, when I'd first arrived, as unusually communal and humane.

In the last few years, however, as the university sank more of its resources into research on new technologies, as it was less supported by the state, and as it increasingly took on the world views of corporations that were funding it, the outlook for small programs like my own had darkened. Several rounds of budget cuts, indeed, and the arrival of a new vice provost had begun to make such programs look expendable. And now a new move to split the College of Letters and Sciences into three distinctive units had thrown the fate of Women's Studies into further question.

The proposed separation into science, social science, and humanities was fine for discipline-based departments like English and Sociology, but faculty in the women's and ethnic studies programs took their approaches from English *and* sociology and from many other disciplines as well. They were interdisciplinary. Where were they supposed to go? That the new vice provost had called a meeting that very day "to discuss the programs' fates" filled me with a sense of dread, and so, reluctantly, I turned my thoughts from squirrels and birds and butterflies to getting ready. When the higher-ups referred to "fate," it was never promising.

I took a final, comforting bite of the tart-sweet scone, still warm and pleasantly rough against my tongue, wrapped its remains in a crumpled Kleenex, and lodged them in my purse. I'd ask the Farmer's Collective Bakery for the recipe. I passed my hand across my mouth to check for crumbs, brushed the front of my blouse where they had landed, and gave my skirt a shake just to be sure they hadn't migrated there as well. I was a messy eater—something having to do with the lack of eye-hand coordination that kept me from playing tennis, ping-pong, golf, and any other game involving the propulsion of small objects to a goal—and it was time to meet with Vice Provost Vogle. I needed to look presentable.

"Emily, wait up." Alma Castillo, director of Chicana/o Studies, hurried across the street, slightly out of breath. "Can you believe it?" she said, her thin brows arching behind a pair of oversized glasses. "How're we going to choose between social science and humanities? We're being forced to take on an identity that doesn't fit. Not that they care." Her rounded cheeks and a head of gray spiked hair gave Alma a piquant, even impish, look.

"Every time there's a crisis in the budget," I said, feeling a familiar warmth in my arms and chest, "we have to justify our right to exist. Never mind that we've poured our lives into developing our programs." I shortened my stride to match Alma's slower one. "And if we're split into different divisions, we'll lose touch with each other. I'd hate to see that happen."

"More and more this place is being run like a corporation. Large departments are becoming larger and strong ones stronger. Too bad about the rest of us." Alma closed her lips in a tight, firm line. "We're like weeds," she said, her lips barely parted, "weeds in their golden fields of corn."

Alma's pale blue blouse, tied at the neck with a soft, loopy bow, made her look like a schoolteacher or a secretary, both of which she had been on her way to her PhD, but, to fashion-conscious me, the way Alma dressed seemed politically strategic. You wouldn't know from looking at her modest blouses and pencil skirts that Alma had been a farm worker and a fierce political organizer in her youth and that she continued to be one of the most outspoken women on campus. I favored out-spoken women, being one myself, and had grown fond of Alma over our years at Arbor State. If I wanted someone to tell me what she really thought, I went to her.

We'd reached the Social Science building—a stark con-figuration of concrete blocks and swooping, science-fiction ramps—where the meeting would take place. The "Deadly Planet," as it was often called, was supposed, in some oblique fashion, to gesture toward the geography of California. Its large rectangles were ostensibly aligned with distant fields; its silver color was intended to suggest the Sierra Nevada mountains, and the curving pathways that joined the blocks together were meant to replicate the paths of winding rivers. Fine on paper, but what about the human part of the natural world?

The building, an experiment in theory and technology, was detached from the needs—and certainly the comforts—of human life. The five-story towers were linked by high external walkways, some of which were grated—much like cattle cross-ings—presenting unsuspecting visitors, and me as well, with vertigo-inducing glimpses of the distant ground below. Inside, the unfinished concrete walls imposed a dungeon-like effect, and many of the hallways either ended without warning or led to doors that were always locked. On my way to meetings in the Deadly Planet, I felt as if I'd stepped into a trap.

"This building is like a maze for laboratory animals."

"*Si,*" Alma said, "and we're the rats."

★ ★ ★

Vice Provost Lorna Vogle, a small woman with short blonde hair, was sitting at one end of a highly polished walnut table as we entered the basement meeting room. We smiled at the four colleagues who'd already arrived and nodded politely to Lorna. She was not a woman to whom we felt close. Lorna was wearing a bright green suit with a green and plum-colored scarf tied artfully around her neck, an outfit that prompted me to gawk at her in wonder. A suit, on a day that would soar into the nineties, and a scarf as well? And the colors! With her long, thin nose, Lorna looked like a hummingbird. But I knew, and not without sympathy for the attempt, that Lorna was determined to appear well turned out—and more. She was bent on projecting a certain perkiness as well, perkiness being a subtle way of expressing spirit, if not authority, with the men who actually ran the show.

Alma and I had barely settled ourselves into our seats when Lorna squared her papers with a series of authoritative taps and began the meeting. I hoped she couldn't tell what I was thinking.

"As you know, your programs will have to choose between being housed in Humanities or in Social Sciences. There are simply no other options."

She paused for effect, coolly surveying the six of us gathered round the table, like someone who'd been trained in crowd control or who'd underlined *The Management Guide to Running Meetings.*

She continued with careful emphasis, "As we make this transition, we need programs that are strong and productive."

I knew that meant departments with high enrollments in their majors and five hundred students squeezed into their lecture rooms, both of which brought monies into the coffers of Arbor State.

"Small programs like your own will have to prove that they are able to keep up. Only strong and productive units will get resources from now on. Weaker programs will have to become part of big departments like English or Sociology."

Outrage burned the veins of my arms and chest and I raised my hand abruptly.

"Emily?" Lorna ruffled slightly with annoyance.

It wasn't time for questions yet, and I knew it.

"Has the university shifted its priorities? Instead of supporting small programs, which provide services that big departments can't and wouldn't want to if they could, have we moved to a system in which only the biggest and strongest survive?"

Lorna placed one hand on her scarf, widened her hazel eyes, and gave me a raptor-like look.

"No, we have not," she said.

Lorna's assistant, a plump, cheery-looking woman, eased her way forward in her seat.

"I think Emily is right. Priorities have shifted in the last few years."

Lorna raised her eyebrows, as if in warning, but then the director of Asian American Studies broke in.

"What needs to be remembered is that we're an advantage to Arbor State. The ethnic studies programs are experts on race and ethnicity and on minority cultures. No other units have that as their goal." He was an older man with thick eyebrows and a wide smile, and he'd devoted twenty years to getting Asian American Studies established on the campus.

"Yes," I said, nodding vigorously in support. "Something similar is true of Women's Studies. And all the programs are crucial in mentoring students who would otherwise be marginalized."

"I'm just telling you what the future is going to look like," Lorna said.

The director of African American Studies, a slender, quiet man from Jamaica, rolled his eyes and then looked down at his papers. The white-haired director of Native American deepened the creases between his brows, and the director of American Studies, a thin slip of a man, tightened his grip on his ballpoint pen as if he'd like to lob it in Lorna's direction. Alma, like a ripening concord grape, visibly swelled with emotion.

"The humanities are also underfunded. This is just the reality." Lorna laced her fingers together on the table, the white tips of her manicure shining like chips of ice, when Alma abruptly launched her upper body forward.

"Well, I guess people in the humanities are second-class citizens, too, much like those of us in women's and ethnic studies."

The director of African American Studies stifled a laugh and then returned to studying his papers. The director of Native American Studies parted his lips as if he'd thought about smiling and then reconsidered it. Lorna's body stiffened ever so slightly behind the table.

"Here's what I want from you in the next two weeks, a report that makes a case for the continued funding of your programs."

The continued funding of our programs? She was threatening our existence right to our faces. I was furious but took notes on her directions nonetheless. Obsessive note taking, or, as I preferred to think of it, keeping track of information, had become second nature ever since I had moved, as a scholarship student, from a working-class town to an upper-class university, where I was so intimidated that I'd written down everything my professors said. Since that time, I'd recorded my impressions about everything—books, lectures, meetings, phone calls, films. It focused my attention, served as a memory bank, and often helped me deal, as now, with unpleasant feelings. I was known on campus as a careful researcher.

After the meeting, the six of us filed out, our faces grim.

"She's threatening to make us disappear." Alma rested one fist on an ample hip.

"We need to meet," I said, looking at the director of Native American Studies, whose usual composure had vanished.

"I'll try to find us a time and reserve us a room." The lines between his eyes had deepened into a scowl.

The directors of Asian American and American Studies nodded their assent. The director of African American shrugged his shoulders in a gesture of habitual weariness, and we all walked on, indignation crackling among us like an electric storm.

"It's all work, low pay, and no respect." Alma paused at the bottom of the stairs, her back against the gray, pockmarked concrete wall. "We're cheap labor, and we're dispensable—we're Mexicans! And when I think about it, I'm Mexican three times over. I'm Mexican. I'm in ethnic studies. And now I'll probably be assigned to the humanities!"

★ ★ ★

The quad stretched before me, a large green rectangle surrounded by cork oak trees and pines. In the early 1900s it had been a field of barley and alfalfa, but now it was a campus lawn where groups of students sprawled on well-trimmed grass. It being noon, some talked or ate their lunches in the shade, others threw Frisbees back and forth in the sunny part of the open space, and just beyond these pastoral borders, faculty and students poured in and out of the student union—like rivulets crossing back and forth in a rock-filled stream. I looked longingly at some tables in the shade but dutifully stationed myself at the bottom of a flagpole that stood at the end of the path dividing the quad in two.

The flagpole area—crowded, baked by sun, and lacking benches—was a lousy place to wait, but I was meeting Tess Ryan of Plant Biology. And like most women in science, she was so busy running a lab and writing grants to support research that she could spare no more than fifteen minutes for a conversation and only in places that didn't take her too far from her work. Collaborating with women scientists often felt like holding a series of conversations with migratory birds. You had to catch them when they had time to perch. And those, like Tess, who were determined to have a family as well as a serious career were particularly hard to snare, although Tess, to her credit, deliberately made time for supporting women's research on campus. She'd even agreed to chair a panel for a Women's Studies lecture series on gender and the environment.

A tall, lean woman with short red hair appeared in the distance, taking long, deep strides and quickly covering the distance between us. Younger than me by at least fifteen years, Tess radiated life. Her tanned skin shone, her eyes looked impossibly clear, and she had the body of an athlete. Standing still, she often reminded me of a young and vigorous stalk of corn. Today, however, she appeared distressed. I gave her what I hoped was a gently inquiring look because what I really wanted to say was "spill the beans."

"Bad things are happening," she said, by way of answer. "One of my colleagues, Peter Elliott, was taken to the hospital this morning in a coma. They found him lying in the hog yard. They think he might have been poisoned."

"In the hog yard?" That seemed an unlikely spot. The hog barn and its yard lay in the science part of campus, but I'd occasionally walked past them—always trying to hold my breath, for the stench they exuded, especially in October's heat, almost smacked you in the face. "What was he doing there?"

"Probably checking on his pigs. He's been feeding them with a genetically modified corn, and he's measuring the rate of their weight gain."

"Do they know how it happened?"

"No." Tess rumpled her forehead. "It could have been food

poisoning, I suppose, but I'm worried, frankly, that it might have involved Save the Fields."

"The group that tore up a graduate student's cornfields before school started?" Save the Fields, I knew, opposed research on genetically engineered crops of any kind. Their preferred mode of protest was to destroy crop fields at night and threaten researchers. "I heard about that." I shook my head. "The corn wasn't even genetically altered."

"Virtually everything we eat is genetically altered in some way. Nature takes care of that." Tess spoke with the patient deliberation one used when one had said something many times before in class. "The crops they tore up were humanly modified using conventional techniques, not genetic engineering, but, despite that fact," Tess's cheeks were turning a peony-like rose, "they've left a note full of threats to everyone working on GMOs." Tess glanced at the crowd around us as if it might conceal suspects.

Tess had reason to be concerned, for she herself worked on genetically modified soybeans. She had strong views about how genetic engineering continued the cross-breeding of plants that farmers had carried on for hundreds of years. Native Americans, she liked to point out, had produced corn by merging different grasses. Genetic engineering was an extension of that process. It frustrated Tess, who cared deeply about using new technologies to feed a hungry world, that people understood so little about the process of breeding plants, not to mention the challenges faced by farmers. She was so smart and so earnest that no one doubted her motives, her politics, or, least of all, her expertise, but not everyone agreed with her point of view. Feelings, I had learned at a panel on GMOs last spring, ran deep on all sides of the issue.

Tess had argued passionately for the right of subsistence farmers to plant GMOs in combating world hunger, although she hadn't been a fan of corporations that didn't care a fig about the fact that subsistence farmers couldn't afford to buy the seeds that biotechnology companies owned. Peter Elliott, with a smugness I found extremely irritating, had stoutly defended Syndicon and its practices with GMOs, while several of my colleagues had vehemently opposed Syndicon and GMOs both.

But was it GMOs themselves or the policies of the corporations that produced them— the relentless focus on profit, the resistance to regulation, the absence of concern for harming, or even helping, others—that my colleagues had really objected to? Did the debate have less to do with GMO technology than with the values it was made to serve? Tess wanted to employ them for global good. Syndicon only cared about its bottom line. The same tension between communal and profit-driven motives had begun to play out all over campus. The threatened downsizing of smaller programs like my own was just one piece of evidence for that.

"Would Save the Fields have actually tried to poison Peter?" I asked. It seemed a long shot to me.

"I don't know, but I'm pretty sure I was followed home last night."

"That's terrible," I said, suddenly envisioning myself in my car at night being pursued by a threatening vehicle. I imagined a dark country road, shadowy fields, no houses in sight, and for a moment the rise and fall of conversation and the bustle of students around me disappeared.

"Did you get a look at the car?"

"It was a dark blue van."

"And you've told the police?"

"I called them as soon as I got home." Tess wasn't someone who was easily intimidated, but I saw that this had scared her.

"What are they doing?"

"They've added security to the fields, instructed us to keep our offices and labs locked up, and told us to report suspicious-looking people hanging around our workplace. But that's not going to help much if someone threatens us off campus." Tess surveyed the crowd once more. "It's awful to live like this."

"I can imagine." Even without menacing notes, I felt uneasy about working evenings at Arbor State. The campus grounds were full of dark expanses; the office buildings, so busy during the day, were empty and dimly lit at night; and incidents of theft and assault had been reported. But what would it feel like to fear, and with plenty of reason, that someone might actually be lying in wait, hidden by shadows, perhaps parked alongside your car in a campus lot? Although there was little reason to think I myself would be singled out, it was deeply unsettling to hear that Tess apparently had. Despite the hot-as-Mojave day, I felt a chill.

I was gazing vacantly at the student union, trying to get my overactive imagination back in line, when I noticed that every table in the union courtyard had been filled. A single bench remained unoccupied. Tess had agreed to moderate a panel on gender and "biodiversity," part of my series on gender and the environment, and "biodiversity" was a concept that I had only begun to understand. If I was going to introduce this panel properly, I needed to know more.

"I know this isn't a good time, but can we sit on the bench for a moment and talk about the panel?"

"Sure," said Tess. "I refuse to stop my life because of threats."

Corn and Cherry Scones

Makes 12–15 scones

2 cups unbleached all-
  purpose flour
½ teaspoon baking soda
1 tablespoon baking
  powder
½ teaspoon kosher salt
⅔ plus ¼ cup sugar

1½ cups medium-grind
  yellow cornmeal
1 cup cold unsalted butter,
  cut into 1-inch cubes
¾ cup dried sweet cherries
1¼ cups buttermilk

Preheat oven to 425°F.

Place the rack in the center of the oven and line 1 or 2 baking sheets with parchment paper.

Sift flour, baking soda, and baking powder into a large bowl. Add salt, ⅔ cup sugar, and the cornmeal, and stir until mixed.

Add butter and cut in with a pastry cutter until the butter is the size of small peas. Mix in the cherries.

Make a well in the center of the mixture and add buttermilk. Mix until ingredients just come together. There will be some loose flour left at the bottom of the bowl.

Let the batter stand for 5 minutes.

Gently shape the dough into balls about 2¼ inches in diameter and place them on the prepared pans about 2 inches apart. The balls should have a rocky exterior.

Sprinkle the ¼ cup sugar on top of the scones. Place them on the middle rack of the oven and immediately turn the temperature down to 375°F.

Bake 20–25 minutes or until the scones are golden. Transfer the scones to a wire rack to cool.

Adapted by permission of the Cheese Board Collective at http:// cheeseboardcollective.coop/. From *The Cheese Board Collective Works* (Berkeley: Ten Speed Press, 2003.)

Chapter 2

A rush of smothering heat enveloped me—like one of the Santa Ana winds I'd grown up with in Southern California. By 3:00 p.m., the temperature in Arborville had shot into the higher nineties, not unusual in mid-October when Indian summer settled in, scorching the whole valley, but after emerging from the pleasant chill of my office in Haven Hall, the initial shock of desert air felt like an assault. Wilting and moving slowly, as if I were a forty-niner crossing Death Valley's shimmering floor, I walked along the quad to Library Lane. It was time for my coffee date with Wilmer Crane, the man who'd answered my ad in the *Valley Bee*.

As I passed a campus parking lot, the sun bouncing off the cars in a dazzling blaze of light, the harsh odor of heated asphalt assailing my nostrils, my thoughts turned to the even more uncomfortable matters of the Hog Barn, the poisoning, and the threatening note. By day, at least, Arbor State had always felt secure, but now, in full sunlight, something disquieting had entered into the atmosphere on campus. Despite the heat, which was further straightening, and surely now frizzing, my hair, I tried to sort it out.

If the poisoning was deliberate, as Tess had feared, was the perpetrator a member of Save the Fields or was it someone on campus who hated Peter's politics? Peter had infuriated a lot of people with his unyielding support of corporate control over GMOs. Some, I realized to my unease, were colleagues I liked and trusted. It was inconceivable to me that any of them had been involved, but was it possible now that some of them might be open to suspicion? The question weighed upon me like the hot, dry air, and I was grateful to reach a row of large old maple trees that shielded me from the sun.

To live in Arborville was to live among large trees. Because the early founders, in their wisdom, had given some thought to the valley heat, Arborville's downtown was lined with large oaks, arching elms, tall cedars, and fragrant pines, giving it a quaint and leafy ambience. Students strolled along the side-walks, bicyclists vied with slow-moving cars in the narrow streets, and dogs, tongues hanging, patiently waited for their owners in the shade.

The buildings were a well-blended mix of old and new—a railroad station with graceful arches in Mission Revival style, dating from the early 1900s; a medium-sized hardware store; a couple of small bookshops; modest dress boutiques, one of which sold the silk underwear I favored; gift shops with iron kitchenware and teacups painted in sunflower designs, which I wasn't partial to; and many casual restaurants. No pharmacist or grocery store, however. For that you had to drive to the outer sections of the town where larger stores were permitted. Arborville, unlike the university it would seem, was protective of its smaller businesses. Students jammed every café with their computers, and the movie house specialized in films for ado-lescent boys, but Arborville had a pleasant, leisurely pace. It was a college town through and through.

As I turned the corner onto Poppy Lane, I began to wonder what my coffee date would be like. His letter had been well written and straightforward. I'd liked him on the basis of that alone, and now, as I descended a set of concrete stairs that led toward a sunken plaza—partially shaded by a feathery foot-hill pine—I saw a man with graying temples sitting at one of the white plastic tables. He had a friendly face with a slightly turned-up nose. There was something open and country-like about him. Good looking, I thought, but what will we say to each other? Having taken languages in college when math and language had been the two choices, I knew nothing of mathematics.

"You must be Wilmer Crane." He held out his hand and I took it. Nice grip, I thought. "I'm Emily Addams. I'll get an iced latte and be back."

"No, let me get it for you."

"Okay, thanks, with nonfat milk, please." Good manners, I observed, as he disappeared inside. There was something about him that reminded me of a country gentleman.

When he returned, I asked, "So, what kind of math do you do?" I wanted to grasp something at least about what the man did. Work meant so much to my own life I couldn't imagine anyone really knowing me without understanding it.

"Chaos theory." Wilmer sat a bit more upright in his chair. He seemed taken aback by my direct interest in his field of study.

"I know almost nothing about math, but could you try to explain that to me in a simple way?"

Wilmer tried, but the words "fractal," "self-iteration," "flows and folding" were unfamiliar to me, a completely foreign tongue. The one thing I did catch was "Butterfly Effect." According to Wilmer, a mathematical talk in 1972 had borne the intriguing title "Does the Flap of a Butterfly's Wings in Brazil Set Off a Tornado in Texas?" Chaos theory maintained that, yes, it could.

"What's chaos theory used for?" I asked.

"All sorts of things. Some people use it to understand the migration of birds and monarch butterflies."

That seemed entirely too difficult to understand. What did it say about a man, I wondered, that he worked on chaos theory? That he was comfortable with complexity? That he needed to control disorder? Both? Neither? Something else? While a slight breeze stirred the needles of the tree, dispersing their piney scent, I paused to consider what question I'd ask him next.

"I had an unsettling experience this morning," Wilmer interjected, turning his sloping blue eyes directly to my face.

His eyes looked big behind his glasses, big in a good way. Definitely good looking, I thought, and smart and tall. I liked a tall man. I found them comforting.

"I went to the Hog Barn this morning. It's next to my office in the Institute for Analytical Dynamics. I was going to do photography for a couple of hours."

Ah, photography, that was something we could talk about.

"I was trying to compose a shot when I saw a man's body lying in the mud next to a pig's pen."

"Peter Elliott?" I leaned across the table and Wilmer nodded. "I heard about him from one of my colleagues. So it was you who found him? He'd ingested poison or something? What'd you do?"

"I jumped in, called for an ambulance, and did CPR. I got him to breathe, but he was still unconscious and he'd thrown up a lot. Then a student appeared out of nowhere and began sobbing like crazy. She was an intern at the Hog Barn, apparently."

"What was her relation to Peter?"

"She fed his pigs."

"She fed his pigs? That's all?"

"It did strike me," Wilmer narrowed his eyes behind his glasses, "that, given the nature of their connection, there was something a bit extreme about her grief."

It struck me that way too.

"What happened next?"

"The emergency workers and police arrived, and I pointed out something odd. He had a piece of corn bread in his hand."

"Corn bread?" I felt my head go light. "How strange. I made corn bread last night, and I took it to campus for a Native American Studies reception in Bauman Hall. That's not far away from the barn. What a weird coincidence." Had there been something wrong with my corn bread? A sudden darkness blossomed in my chest. "But I ate the bread and so did a lot of people," I said, more to myself than to Wilmer. "No one got sick that I know of. I didn't, and I always get ill if there's something wrong with food. I didn't see Peter at the reception, and, anyway, I doubt he'd even know about it."

"Well," Wilmer bent toward me with a comforting look, "we don't know that it *was* your corn bread. Lots of people make corn bread, and he could have bought some just about anywhere. Let's not jump to conclusions."

"You're right, but still, how curious." I stared blankly for a moment at the gray and russet sparrows rustling and pecking at crumbs near our feet. Could my corn bread really have gotten mixed up in this mess? I tried for a moment to think of other yellow foods. Corn muffins? Corn scones? Corn pudding? Or wait, pigs ate corn too. Had his hand been full of feed for hogs?

"Are you sure it was corn bread, not pig food or something else that was yellow?"

"It wasn't pig food, that's for sure."

I glanced at the sparrows again, trying to recall details from the gathering I'd attended the night before, and when I raised my head, I saw that Wilmer was studying me.

"What do *you* work on?"

He seemed eager to put the Hog Barn and its memories behind us. Perhaps they cast me in a disturbing light? Some first meeting, now that I thought about it. His date turns out to be a suspect in an attempted poisoning! "Coincidentally enough, I'm writing about dishes made of corn, about their cultural meanings. I used to be in literature, but when I came to Arbor

State, I decided to work on popular culture. Recently I decided to write some pieces on food."

Wilmer nodded.

"And baking is part of your investigation?"

"I wanted to write on a subject that would connect my work with my personal life, and I wanted to know my subject in different ways, not just through conventional research but through cooking and eating and ways I don't even know about yet." He was a mathematician. How was I going to explain the nature of my research? "Besides, I like to cook, and my daughter likes to cook with me. It's something fun we can do together." That was no better.

I studied my hands resting on the table and adjusted one of my silver and turquoise rings. I was fond of turquoise. Then I looked straight at Wilmer. "I give a lot of food-based parties, and I guess you could say I'm obsessed with bringing food to gatherings and also with thinking about the role of food in building relationships and community." I stopped short.

Wilmer tilted his head and narrowed his eyes once more. Maybe I'd looked like that when he'd described the Butterfly Effect.

"Given your work," I said, "this must seem foreign to you."

"Not really." He paused as if giving the matter some thought. "Chaos theory has relevance for ordinary, day-to-day life. It's used in analyzing weed control, in setting the price of pigs— and even in growing corn."

I was pleased that Wilmer's math had such down-to-earth and, potentially, community-minded applications, though I couldn't imagine how they would work. Having never gotten beyond algebra and geometry, I found higher math a total mystery.

The sun moved beyond the top of the Redbud Café, deepening the shade.

"Have you been married?" I was keen on turning us away from the disturbing issue of my corn bread.

"Yes." Wilmer blushed. "Twice. And both times they left me. My last wife went off with someone else six months ago. How about you?"

"It's been a year since my marriage broke up," I replied. Why had the wives left? Don't ask, I told myself firmly, not at our first meeting. Instead, I inquired if he had children. He had two boys, both of them on their own. I told him about Polly, and then as the heat of the day broke, I glanced at my watch. "I have to pick up my daughter. I've enjoyed our time."

The tables had emptied and the plaza had fallen into shadow when Wilmer unfolded himself from his plastic chair.

"Would you like to do this again?"

"Sure." I definitely did want to do this again.

"Do you think we'll have enough to talk about?" He watched me closely as I gathered my things.

"I guess we'll see." I smiled with encouragement. I hoped that would be the case, and I was fairly certain we'd find things to talk about. But, then again, I'd never dated a man in mathematics.

★ ★ ★

I stood in my kitchen with its white walls and its border of coral and turquoise tile. I was nuts about New Mexico and had turned a worn 1960s ranch house into a vision of Santa Fe with Mexican pavers on the floor, a fake adobe half wall dividing the kitchen from the dining room, and carved animals—rabbits, pigs, and donkeys in yellows, pinks, and browns—peering out from bookcases and down from the tops of cabinets. I figured my love for Santa Fe had had its origins in early childhood when I had lived in a small adobe house in the middle of a California desert. Maybe Santa Fe was my early life as I wished it could have been—vibrant, colorful, sensuous—not to mention my current life as I was always wanting it to be.

My daughter, Polly, was at my side stirring polenta in a

large white pot. We were going to experiment with a deli-
cious-sounding dish: polenta, dry Sonoma jack cheese, tomato
fondue, and lots of cream.

"How's the polenta going?" I peered over her shoulder into
the thickening yellow mush.

"I think it's ready to go into the pan."

When I looked at Polly with her corkscrews of long, brown
hair and large blue eyes, much larger than mine, my chest filled
with light. I loved these evenings at home with my daughter.
They were an excuse to be fully human, as I thought of it.
When Polly and our dog, Sadie, were there, the house felt full
of life. When they were gone, I accomplished far more work,
but the two of them haunted the place, making me long for
their vibrancy and for their cheerful demands on my attention.

"Okay, let me lift the pot—it's heavy. Then you can spread
the polenta on the jelly roll pan." I poured the hot polenta
onto the rimmed metal sheet and Polly smoothed it into the
corners. "Great, I'll pick the tomatoes for the fondue. Maybe
you want to do a little homework now before it gets too late?"
I'd mastered the mother's strategy of suggesting, rather than
imposing, tasks.

"Okay, but tell me when the tomatoes are done. I want to
help layer everything." Polly went to her room.

"Go on, Sadie," I said to the dog. "You go with Polly.
Help her with her work." Solomon and I had given Polly a
puppy when we divorced, and now Sadie, a golden retriever of
immense goodwill, accompanied Polly back and forth in a joint
custody arrangement, spending every other day with me and
splitting weekends between me and Polly's father. Solomon and
I had at least worked out a mutually agreeable set of arrangements for our daughter. We were much better divorced than we
had been while married.

Nonetheless, I often worried that the divorce had hurt Polly
far more than she let on, that there was a wound in her that

I could only guess at and never see, and that made me especially glad for Sadie, who was a comforting spirit in Polly's life. She slept at Polly's side in both parental houses, her four legs stretching from the top to the bottom of the bed, her tawny golden head commandeering her own pillow. Polly adored her, and she was a true companion animal, a reassuring bridge between the pieces of Polly's divided home lives.

I opened the dining room sliders and entered the quiet of the yard. Off to the side lay a vegetable garden where full red tomatoes and pale green tomatillos lingered. Black figs hung heavily, like wrinkled pouches, upon the large tree. I could smell their winey ripeness. Song swallows made warbling sounds. A hummingbird whirred in the air feeding on purple salvia, and a bronze monarch silently winged its way past. I listened to the quiet. The garden surged with life, and I was a part of it, receiving and tending to it. But all the while it went on without me. It felt healing after the brutal developments on campus—the meeting with Lorna, the news of the poisoning and of the threat to Tess, and now the troubling idea that my corn bread could have played a role in the Hog Barn incident.

Back inside the kitchen as I heated water for peeling the tomatoes, my anger at Lorna rose to the surface, but in less acute form. I knew women administrators had it hard. No matter what they really thought, they were there to do the bidding of the upper administration, which, on a campus that had once devoted itself to agriculture and then to science and technology, consisted almost entirely of men whose main concern was science. Women administrators were expected to outperform their male peers, but if their ideas failed to accord with those of their superiors, they didn't last long. They went on "extended leave," were shuttled to the system's head office, and sometimes seemed to disappear, their desk cleared off, overnight. One female vice provost who'd been sympathetic to

Women's Studies had found life so difficult that she'd left after only three years in office.

That vice provost had taken the concerns of Women's Studies seriously, had attempted to exert influence on the higher-ups, had seemed to empathize with the program's sense of being embattled, and had tried, in a discreet way, to be sisterly. I felt her absence. Not that all male administrators were indifferent. I had worked with several who understood and sympathized with the program, treating it with generosity and respect. Thank God, for them. But Lorna, in contrast, had shown little interest in the program and, worse, had seemed determined to use a heavy hand. Telling us that only big departments would survive. It stung more when coming from another woman.

I plopped the tomatoes into the pot and watched them boil. Cooking soothed me, turned my thoughts to more harmonious matters. I thought of how cooking connected me to one of my oldest friends, Miriam, whose dinners, however simple, had always seemed so elegant. It was Miriam who had instilled in me a passion for cooking and Miriam's dining rooms—some golden yellow, some aubergine—that had inspired me to use color in a bold and thoughtful way. Soon, I realized, it would be the sixth anniversary of Miriam's death—from a brain tumor at only thirty-four. Perhaps that's why she'd been on my mind so much lately, Miriam—and the nagging sense that I could have done more for her in her illness. She'd lived on the other side of the country, in rural upstate New York, and though I'd sent her money every month, if I'd called or written more often . . . Remorse clutched me in its grip. At least, I'd finally made the long journey to see her, had cooked pepper steak in cognac sauce according to her exact instructions, had stayed up with her talking, laughing, and drinking wine until long past midnight. It had been like old times. A week later, quite suddenly, Miriam was dead.

"Polly," I called, at last, "I think we're ready to layer." I cut the firmed polenta into strips. Polly lay one strip in the but-tered baking dish, I spooned on the tomato mixture, and Polly added the shaved dry Sonoma jack. We repeated the process until all the polenta strips were used. I poured cream over the top and slid the dish into the oven. The kitchen began to smell of bubbling tomato, melting cheese, and baking corn, though now the very smell of corn, in all its sweetness, brought me back to the corn bread in Peter Elliott's hand. Was it the corn bread I had made for the reception? Had someone put it to a dark purpose and, if so, how would I find out? I struggled to keep the disconcerting thoughts from diminishing my usual pleasure in the kitchen.

Oven Polenta, Tomato Fondue, and Sonoma Jack Cheese

Polenta

4 tablespoons unsalted butter

½ medium onion, minced fine

1 cup large cracked polenta (Golden Pheasant if possible)

1 tablespoon coarse salt

1 teaspoon cracked black pepper

4 cups boiling water

Tomato Fondue

1 tablespoon unsalted butter

¼ cup extra-virgin olive oil

2 medium shallots, minced

1 medium garlic clove, minced

1½ pounds tomatoes (peeled, seeded, and finely chopped; about 3–4 medium tomatoes)

1 tablespoon tomato paste

¼ bay leaf

1 tablespoon sugar

Salt and pepper

Other Ingredients

6 ounces dry Sonoma Jack cheese, shaved (must be dry and the quality is important)

1½ cup heavy cream

Assembly

Preheat oven to 350°F.

Melt butter in an ovenproof pan. Add the onion and sauté over low heat about 5 minutes until translucent.

Remove from heat and add the polenta, stirring. Add salt and pepper to boiling water and pour it over the polenta, mixing lightly. Bake in the pot for 30 minutes until the polenta is firm but liquid enough to be spread.

Spread the polenta on an oiled 10 by 15-inch jelly roll pan, smoothing the top. You should have a ½-inch layer. Cool and refrigerate, covering the top. May be done two days in advance.

Place butter and olive oil in skillet over medium heat. Sauté shallots about 5 minutes until translucent. Add the remaining ingredients and simmer 20 minutes. Salt and pepper to taste and remove bay leaf.

Butter an 8-inch square pan and smear the bottom with some of the fondue. Cut the cold polenta into 8 strips about 7½ by 3½ inches. Place the first strip against one side of the dish. Spoon fondue along the side that touches the edge of the dish. Sprinkle cheese onto the line of fondue. Overlap the next polenta strip so that it just covers the line of fondue and cheese. Proceed until you have used all the strips.

Drizzle cream over all and bake until the top is golden and bubbly, about 35–40 minutes.

Adapted by permission of Gary Danko from *Lee Bailey's California Wine Country Cooking* (New York: Clarkson Potter/Publishers, 1991).

Chapter 3

The next day, I was pushing at the door of the women's bathroom on the second floor of Haven Hall when Isobel Flores-Rivera strode around the corner. Isobel, professor of Native American Studies, maintained a whirlwind of a schedule. She often directed her department, closely mentored her students, sat on multiple college committees, chaired the Latina Council, and helped out at the Native American university nearby. Even with that schedule, however, you could trust Isobel to get things done. I liked that kind of person. I was known as a workhorse too.

Isobel's strong-featured face, surrounded by long, dark hair, looked for the moment, like a thundercloud about to open.

"Emily, I was coming to see you."

"Come in with me. I have to go." We entered the bathroom, and I peered carefully under the two stalls. The room smelled sharply of cleaning liquid, but no one else was there. I quickly used one of the toilets.

"What's up?" I asked, washing my hands and drying them on one of the university's scratchy brown paper towels.

"The police came to Frank's office this morning."

"Frank? What for?" Frank Walker, a retired professor and an elder in Native American Studies, still came to his office and was uncommonly vocal politically. He made a habit of e-mailing the entire campus, including the top administration, about the university's increasingly corporate values, about the real meaning of ecology, and about injustices at Arbor State, of which there were many. The administration never followed his advice, as far as I could tell, but he had an integrity they had to admire. He was well known on campus and treated with respect.

"Attempted murder it would seem." Isobel scowled. "Did you hear about Peter Elliott in the Hog Barn?"

"Yes, I did. So they don't think the poisoning was accidental?" I felt the darkness reenter my bosom.

Isobel shook her head.

"Seemingly not or why would they have questioned Frank?"

"Why on earth *did* they question Frank?"

"He was up before dawn on Monday morning heading toward the creek and the arboretum for his meditative walk, and someone, I don't know who, saw him near the Hog Barn." Isobel's face tightened. "Of course, it would be one of us they'd suspect. They take our land, and then they treat us like *we're* the invasive species!" It was rumored that the university had been built on Native burial grounds.

"Corn bread was found in Peter's hand," I said. "Had you heard about that? I'd brought some to the reception Sunday evening before Frank spoke."

"Was that yours? It was good." Her face softened briefly. "But there can't be a connection between your corn bread and Peter, at least not through Frank."

"The police might think so, however." I folded my arms and leaned against one of the bathroom's pale tan walls. It felt uncomfortably cool through my thin blouse. "Frank and Peter went at it on that panel about GMOs last spring. Peter completely took the corporate line. And Frank argued at length about how corporations steal Native knowledge and plant materials and then patent what they do with them and make massive profits. 'Bio' piracy' he called it, another way of occupying what Native Americans had first."

"But they questioned Frank because he'd been seen near the Hog Barn, not because of some panel on GMOs."

"You're right. Someone would have had to tell them about the panel, though I can't imagine who. Did they ask Frank about the reception?"

"They drilled him about where he'd been for the last twenty-four hours. And when he told them about the reception, they asked him if food had been served there, and when he said yes, they questioned him about corn bread. He remembered the corn bread but didn't know who'd made it. They didn't tell him why they'd asked. Now, I see the connection."

I stared down for a moment at the bathroom's beige-tiled floor. Frank had grown up in a dingy Southern California town, but he'd had a strong connection to rural life. He liked to recall how baby ducks had followed him, how he'd loved plants and other living things, how he'd felt a child of nature. He was a poet and a visionary and, though, like everyone, he had his eccentricities, I'd always known him to be generous and open to working with others outside his own program. Now, my corn bread might have put him in an awkward, even dangerous, spot.

"Isobel." I looked up at her. "Did you have any bad effects from eating the corn bread?"

"No, and I didn't hear of anyone else who got sick." She turned on the tap and began to wash her hands, slowly, as if they too might be polluted.

"Then if it was my corn bread, it wasn't food poisoning. Did someone put something in the corn bread I left and then feed it to Peter?" The corn bread had been meant as an offering, a contribution to the community represented by the gathering. Had someone turned it to a bad end? To me, providing food was a gesture of hospitality and eating it, an act of trust. I'd always thought of sharing meals as a way of bringing people together across the things that otherwise divided them. But now, the whole meaning of my gift might have been turned on its head. Feeling weak, I rested my heavy turquoise purse on the ledge in front of the bathroom mirror.

"I should go to the police and tell them I made it."

"I would." Isobel dried her hands on another rough towel. "There might be more bad corn bread out there, and maybe the police will tell you if the corn bread they found had the ingredients you used. Remember, we don't know yet that it *was* your corn bread. Lots of people make corn bread. I make it with blue cornmeal or with cranberries. The Iroquois boiled theirs."

"This had caramelized onions and goat cheese."

"I'll have to try that."

Both of us looked in the mirror. Isobel smoothed her bright turquoise T-shirt over her black skirt. She was fond of colors that threw her dark eyes and hair into vivid relief. She wore no makeup and didn't need it. I powdered my nose and reapplied my eyeliner and lipstick. For some reason my makeup always disappeared after a few hours, making me look disturbingly pale.

"So the police suspect Frank of being involved. It's hard to fathom."

"Since they questioned him, I guess they do. But, if it *was* your corn bread—I'm telling you this as a friend—everyone at the reception is now a suspect."

I sighed out loud. I'd worked hard over the years doing my part in bringing the women's and ethnic studies programs together, and now a simple, friendly act on my part had placed people I cared for under suspicion.

"Keep me posted, will you?" I said. "I'm going to tell the police and see if there's a match."

Isobel and I were now close, although once that hadn't been true. Isobel had taken me to task publicly, painfully about my interpretation of a film involving Native Americans. Most distressingly, it was a reading with which I had assumed Isobel would empathize and agree. For at least a year she'd been impossible to approach. But I'd kept trying and finally confronted her and explained the reading, and Isobel had understood what I'd been trying to say. For that year, Isobel said, her strategy had been to react to everything that offended her with anger, but now her strategy had changed.

Since that time I had come to cherish Isobel not just as someone who had a powerful presence and got things done, but as someone caring, large-hearted, and full of life, as someone skilled in the healing arts. Once, when I had been upset over a hostile administrative move, Isobel had taught me how to dissipate my anger.

"Imagine a line from you to the person you have anger toward. Imagine a light burning up the line. Imagine a flash at the other end."

I was going to have more and more use for a practice like that—or so it seemed.

★ ★ ★

I sat at my desk with no appetite for class preparations. After Isobel's revelation about Frank Walker, I had to think about the gathering I'd attended on Sunday evening. The Native American reception had been held in a large seminar room in Bauman Hall. I remembered that one wall of the room had been colored a soft coral and that one of the long walls had been painted with a mural showing folk-like pasturelands, sheep, and cows. Faculty in Animal Science, where the seminar was located, had a sense of playfulness that I appreciated. The few times I'd been to Bauman and had had to ask directions, male faculty had answered me and guided me in a friendly, even jolly, way. I thought that caring about animals might have made them extra friendly to living species in general. Perhaps, men like that had been at the center of the university's traditional communal spirit.

There had been candles in the room that evening, giving it a soft, inviting bloom, and Isobel had smudged me soon after my arrival with a smoldering bunch of dried grasses that smelled of sage. Smudging was offered to everyone who attended gatherings like this. It was a way of asking the plant spirits to cleanse you of negative energy. Isobel had first waved the sharp herbal smoke to the four directions, calling for blessing and protection, and then she had fanned the smoke around me as I faced her, passing the wand back and forth, starting at my feet and moving upward.

"Turn away from me," Isobel had said and then she passed the wand down my back. I, being sensitive to energy work of any kind, felt something in me shift. Was it the smoke, the plant spirits, the care that Isobel expressed through this ritual, or Isobel's own energy that made me feel suddenly clearer in mind and lighter in spirit than I'd been before? Maybe all of it combined.

Frank had given a speech, wearing a corduroy jacket, a white shirt, and a bolo tie, his dark, gray-streaked hair tied back in a ponytail, his prominent nose as sharp as the edge of a carved stone. He'd welcomed guests to the reception and had launched into a meditation about the nature of community. He'd spoken about ecology as a way of thinking about life that brought together the sacred source of creation with plants, animals, human beings, and the light of the sun.

"We do nothing by ourselves. We are part of a continuum extending outward from our consciousness, living in harmony with living things. Even rocks are living energy." Frank paused and took the room in. It had grown quiet as he spoke. Although there was no central Native American doctrine, the Native way, as he had experienced it, was to live with gratitude and humility.

"Humility and lack of arrogance are accompanied by a tendency toward simplicity of living, and that reinforces the ideal of concentrating on the ethical quality of one's life as opposed to focusing on competition and amassing personal possessions."

Frank's ecology, I reflected, seemed a more spiritual version of what Tess had called biodiversity. Both ways of thinking assumed the connectedness of all to all, both valued the smallest forms of life for what they contributed to the whole. Lorna's emphasis on big departments and her threats about making small programs disappear represented a stark contrast in worldview. I liked to hear Frank talk. He made me feel more humble and yet more alive, more aware of the life around me. He touched something deep within me, reminded me of what was important. Now Frank looked at each quadrant of the room. It was ceremonial, not quite like church, which I'd attended as a child, but close.

"We must see ourselves as part of the earth, not as an enemy from outside who tries to impose its will on it. We cannot hurt any part of the earth without hurting ourselves." And then he'd cited Slow Buffalo, from a thousand years ago: "'The sky is your father, the earth is your grandmother. Whatever grows in the earth is your mother. Always remember your grandmother is underneath your feet.' The first thing an Indian learns is to love each other."

Could a man who talked like that poison anyone? Sitting in my office now, staring at the European elms outside my window, I couldn't imagine it.

★ ★ ★

Home again that afternoon, I'd slipped into my study chair, a cup of decaf on my desk, the swimming pool—a common feature of Arborville's sweltering backyards—reflecting blue-green light through the French doors, when a solid knock on the door and a determined ringing of the front bell cut through my solitude. I opened the front door curiously. No one knocked on my door unless they were trying to sell me something, often their own religion. Two female police officers stood outside in their blue uniforms, one tall, one short.

"Are you Professor Addams?" the smaller of them asked. I nodded. "I'm Sergeant Gina Garcia," she said, holding herself tightly. "Sergeant Dorothy Brown," said the other who was broader and whose arms hung loosely at her sides. Her skin was the color of French espresso.

"Can we come in? We'd like to ask you some questions," Sergeant Brown said. Her uniform enlarged her already wide frame.

"Sure. Please, come in and have a seat." I led the women to the dining table that looked onto the pool, and the three of us seated ourselves delicately.

Sergeant Brown removed her hat, revealing a close cap of gray hair, while I perched uneasily on my chair. I hadn't planned to call the police until later that afternoon, needing time to figure out what I would say. Would it look bad that I hadn't called sooner? I knew it would, and Sergeant Garcia, with her thin face and dark hair pulled tightly under her cap, looked severe.

"We want to ask you about a reception you attended on Sunday evening," Sergeant Brown said.

"Yes, it was the Native American welcome reception. I was there." Having delayed my call, I was determined now to be as forthright as possible.

"And had you done some baking for the reception?"

"I'd made corn bread with caramelized onions and goat cheese."

Dorothy's square face took on a sudden nostalgic look.

"I've never had it like that," she said. "It sounds good."

"Me neither," Gina said, removing her own hat. "I've had it with jalapeños."

She was so petite that her uniform might have come from

the boy's department. Good, I thought. They both like food. But would that help? I couldn't tell.

"My mother used to make the best corn bread," Dorothy continued. "She'd put some butter in a skillet and get it all hot, then pour the batter in and put the skillet in the oven. That skillet gave it a nice crust." Dorothy looked for a moment at the pool outside, her substantial hands lying on the table before her. They seemed like capable hands, hands used to taking care of business. I imagined Dorothy at a stove, stirring something in a pot, her high-cheekboned face, with a faraway look, pointed toward a window. But really, I caught myself, is this what we should be doing, day-dreaming about cooking?

"Did you eat the corn bread?" Gina asked, with a sharp look for Dorothy.

"Yes, I did and so did a colleague of mine."

"And you had no bad side effects?"

"No, none, and if there's something wrong with food, I always get sick. I don't have a great stomach. My colleague was fine too."

"What did you put into it?" Gina was about to write in a small notebook.

"Cornmeal, baking powder, flour, buttermilk, honey, eggs, corn, the onions, and goat cheese."

"Was this cornmeal you had at home?" I nodded. "And you'd baked with it before and you were fine?"

"Yes, there was nothing bad about the cornmeal that I know."

"Is there any way someone could have put something into the corn bread without your knowing it?" Gina's pen hovered above the notebook.

"I left the reception early and I took my platter and left the rest of the bread on paper plates. So I guess someone could have taken it away after I was gone." I turned my palms up on the table. The idea that someone at this reception, in particular, could have turned my corn bread into a weapon was disturbing. Who'd been there? Frank, Isobel, Antonio Conti, the director of the program, other faculty I knew well, and a young half-Native, half-Chicano professor I'd met at the GMO panel. There'd been graduate and undergraduate students as well, many of them white. And then the staff.

"Do you remember who was at the reception?" Dorothy asked.

"Colleagues and staff I know, but plenty that I didn't. I imagine Frank Walker has a better idea than I have. I assume it was you who talked to him."

Dorothy and Gina sat silent.

"We can't comment on that," Gina said. "Did you know Professor Elliott?"

"I'd met him once."

"Do you know anyone who might want to harm him?"

"Not really."

Then Gina asked me where I'd gone after the reception and where I had spent the early morning hours.

"I drove straight home and was asleep by eleven and up again by eight the next morning." My schedule was boringly predictable.

"We'd like to search your kitchen. If you'd sign this agreement for us to do so, it will save time and we won't have to get a search warrant."

Search the kitchen? This was getting serious. But I nodded and signed. I couldn't imagine them finding anything suspicious in my kitchen. And wasn't cooperating with the police, in this case, the best thing to do?

"We'll need to take the cornmeal, the platter, and the pan and any other ingredients you have left over," Gina continued.

I found the platter, pan, cornmeal, baking soda, flour, and honey.

"I'm afraid I used all the goat cheese, onions, buttermilk, and corn."

"Thanks," Dorothy said. "I'm afraid we'll still have to search." The two women put on latex gloves and began methodically opening and closing the white cabinets and drawers with soft clacks. Then they searched my garbage can, taking out some wrappers and sealing them in plastic bags. This was the kind of thing I'd seen on television crime shows. It felt unreal, even dreamlike, but in a nightmare sort of way, to see two strangers going through my kitchen.

I took some comfort in the fact that my spices were lined up in alphabetical order, the glasses, plates, and silverware stacked neatly in cupboards and drawers, the kitchen utensils corralled in a turquoise crock. Even the garbage can had not yet developed a sour smell. Surely, this spoke well of my character. And at least, the police had sent two people who seemed respectful of the space, seemed to understand that searching a woman's kitchen was an act of intimacy that required a delicate touch. Would other officers, male officers perhaps, have felt that kind of empathy? Would Wilmer? I'd not been thinking about Wilmer much. There was a lot going on.

"Thanks for your help," Dorothy said, when they were finished. The two women removed their gloves. "We may be back, and if you think of anyone who would want to harm Professor Elliott, please let us know."

"I will, but do you know for certain that it was my corn bread that was found in Peter's hand?"

"No, we won't have the lab results for several days, but now that you've given us the ingredients we'll let the lab know what to look for." Gina and Dorothy exited the door.

Geez, I thought, this could cure me of bringing food to gatherings. Now I and everyone else at the reception was a potential suspect. Had any baking project ever gone so wrong? But was it *my* corn bread? Maybe Wilmer and Isobel were right. Lots of people made corn bread, and it was easy to buy. I'd seen a bakery table with corn bread on it in the farmer's market just last week.

Southern Corn Bread

½ stick butter

¾ cup yellow corn meal

¾ cup general all-purpose flour

1 tablespoon baking powder

½ teaspoon sea salt

½ cup sugar

1 egg

¼ cup milk

Put a cast iron skillet in a cold oven and preheat to 350°F. Once the oven is at the right temperature, put the butter in the hot skillet and return it to the oven.

In a large bowl, whisk together your dry ingredients (cornmeal, sugar, flour, baking powder, and salt). In a small bowl, whisk together the egg and milk until fully incorporated.

Make a well in the center of your dry ingredients and pour your wet ingredients in and mix with a rubber spatula. Do not overmix. Lumps are fine. Add most of the hot butter to the mixture and mix a bit more. Again, do not overmix.

Pour the mixture into the hot skillet and bake for about 20–30 minutes, until nicely browned and a toothpick inserted into the cornbread comes out mostly dry with some damp crumbs.

Recipe by kind permission of Mattie Smith Nettles.

Chapter 4

Haven Hall was a graceful, buff-colored building with a red tile roof and large windows that actually opened—it had been built in the 1920s before university buildings had been designed to hermetically seal in their occupants. I loved its spaciousness and its light and the fact that it housed women's, American, and the four ethnic studies programs. Some of the programs' offices were mixed together, and the place seemed less like a worksite than like a neighborhood, where people gathered together in the halls, visited each other's offices, and sometimes met in the women's bathroom to discuss important strategies.

The main staircase, however, had an acrophobia-inducing well that extended from the third to the bottom floor, and I tried not to look down it at the floor below. Once, in Colorado's Mesa Verde Park, Solomon and I had sat with a tour group on a ledge that overlooked a deep canyon. I couldn't see the canyon from my position on the ledge, where I had planted myself against a rough rock wall, but I'd known it was there, and I'd grown so faint that I'd had to grip Solomon's arm to stave off the sensation of plunging into distant crevasses below. Climbing the stairs this morning, I kept my eyes directly in front of me.

At the top of the staircase, doors opened to a conference room that was shared by all the programs in the building.

A long rectangle with floor-to-ceiling windows and a view of the tops of bushy trees, it was my favorite place to meet, like being in a canopy, a refuge within the refuge that Haven Hall itself provided. Despite the light and greenery, however, the mood of the meeting would be tense. Faculty from the ethnic, American, and women's studies programs were coming together to respond to Lorna's threats, only three days ago, about cutting our funding or possibly merging us into English or Sociology. Given what I'd heard about the gender troubles in one department and the turf wars in the other, the choices felt bleak. Which was better? Falling from a cliff or tumbling down a well?

Since the director, Antonio Conti, was away, Isobel took the floor as soon as we'd settled in.

"It's their old corporate trick. For years they've tried to collapse the ethnic studies programs into a single unit, which would have allowed them to cut staff positions, double the workload of the remaining staff, and reallocate the money to the sciences. The new tactic is to scatter us between Social Sciences and Humanities, starve us, merge us into a larger department, fire our staff, and then watch us disappear. That we're mainly white women and women and men of color only makes it easier to justify their policies. They're used to regarding us as marginal."

"We should consider some kind of unification," Alma called out. "Why not become a separate division of Ethnic, Women's, and American Studies?"

"Excellent thought," the director of Asian American said.

"We could ask for our own dean," I added. Where was this going?

Isobel, striking in a purple T-shirt and long black skirt, moved like a dancer to the board.

"Why don't we list the things we all want for our programs."

Something new was in the air. None of the programs had ever contemplated uniting.

"To get support for our programs and research units."

"To turn out students who are human beings, who can think critically, and who want to change the world."

"Not to be competitive with each other, to have community."

One by one everyone in the room was enlarging the list as Isobel's chalk tap-tapped against the board.

I was taking notes as fast as I could. I, along with Alma, Isobel, Frank, and the directors of the American and the ethnic studies programs, had worked hard toward bringing our faculty together. We'd tried to build relationships by showing up at each other's lectures and conferences, having coffee together, dropping by each other's offices, talking out conflict, and enjoying each other's company at my large off-campus buffets. Being part of this community-building effort was important to me politically, but it had also helped fill the void that had been left by Miriam's death. The community itself, indeed, had supplied a sense of home that was continually being disrupted in the domestic space I shared with Solomon. It was comforting that a community could feel so much like family, and, for political and deeply personal reasons both, I was devoted to its survival.

Still, I'd never imagined a moment like this. Each of our units would retain its separate identity, but we'd change our informal circle into a formal structure. It was more than I'd ever hoped for. I remembered an angry moment earlier in our days when a volatile professor of Native American Studies and an equally volatile professor in Chicana/o Studies had gotten into an argument and suddenly jumped from their seats, as if about to come to blows. We'd come a long way from eruptions such as those.

"Isobel," Alma said, "why don't you write up a proposal for our becoming a separate division? Then we can meet again and go over it." Time was short. The reorganization of Letters and Sciences was going forward, and the deadline for responses to the administration's plan was a little more than a week away. We had to move quickly or our fates would be decided for us—by Vice Provost Vogle.

"How about an evening meeting?" Isobel suggested.

"I'll volunteer my house," I said. I'd noticed that everyone felt freer and bolder when meetings were held off campus.

★ ★ ★

I stayed in my office that evening e-mailing about the faculty's winter schedules, though I usually avoided working after hours in Haven Hall. It was isolated at night on the upper floors, and because of the computer lab on the first, the main doors were left unlocked. Anyone could walk the halls at night, which gave late-working staff the creeps, and the place was poorly illuminated as well. But this was the night of the fall reception for the Latina Council, and there was no point in going home and then driving back. Since Alma was in her office just around the corner, I had her company and, later, we could walk over together to the Deadly Planet, where Isobel had somehow convinced the administration to give her a series of rooms for the council's offices. Isobel could be very persuasive.

I'd had coffee with Alma two weeks after I'd moved to Arborville. Hired to develop the Women's Studies program, I'd taken seriously the criticism by women of color that women's studies was too white and middle-class and had promised myself not to let that happen at Arbor State. From the beginning, I'd devoted my energies, and much of my heart, to creating a program that was half white, half women of color and to consolidating ties among the women's and the ethnic studies programs. From the start, Alma had been welcoming and more. She'd been ready to be friends and had helped me organize a series of lectures on different kinds of feminisms that had made a strong beginning for our community-building work. That was another thing I liked about Alma. She was always ready to join forces.

Now a little before seven, I knocked on her door and she opened, the walls behind her covered with Chicana/o art and political posters. One showed a black fist raising a string of barbed wire inside a red circle. That was Alma. Bold. But one look at her this evening gave me a start—her forehead was creased, her pale green cardigan askew, and her hair unusually upright as if it had been pulled sharply toward the heavens.

"Are you okay?" I wasn't used to seeing Alma in distress.

"I'm having some trouble with one of my junior faculty. She's working against the promotion of another colleague and she shouldn't be."

"Why would she do that?"

"She's out for herself."

Alma was being discreet but I guessed who it was—a new faculty member who was intense, ambitious, and eager to take over whatever looked promising to her own career. Even in small programs, not everyone thought the same way and not everyone was interested in working on each other's behalf. In Women's Studies, as well, a new hire had begun to act like a diva. Fortunately, she was away doing research on the thorny concept of gender, and the program was palpably more peaceful in her absence.

"We have enough problems with the administration. It doesn't help to have faculty working against each other." Alma closed the door to her office. "Sometimes I feel like a mother with too many children."

"I know the feeling." I'd directed my own program for several years.

We walked out of Haven Hall, crossing in front of the student union, and then down a dusky sidewalk.

"That was a great idea you had at the meeting about forming a unified front."

"There's strength in numbers. You know, 'The People United . . .'"

"'. . . Will Never Be Defeated.'"

"It's not always true, but it's true enough, and what else do we have? You have to stick with your allies and your goals. I learned that early on."

We headed down a still-darker pathway. "When my mother and father worked in the fields near Allenville, the town where I grew up, they were constantly harassed by *La Migra*. One day some officers told my father to go back to Mexico, and he said, 'You'll have to take me at the point of a gun. This is my homeland and I can't leave it.' They let him go."

Alma was full of such motivating stories.

"My family used to drive through Allenville on our way to relatives farther east," I said. "It wasn't much of a town back then."

"I couldn't wait to get out of there. My brothers fought, drank, and smoked when they were young. They lived it up and then became pillars of the community. But girls like me were kept behind locked doors to protect their virtue. I used to say '*Nací para ser rebelde.*' I was born to be rebellious."

I found it hard to imagine Alma behind locked doors. Instead, I could feel her determination lifting me, the way that winds sometimes buoy you up in dreams. Perhaps we *could* present a united front and save our programs. Perhaps we *could* sustain community in the face of the competitive, me-first, money-driven culture that had been creeping into a university that had once seemed just the opposite.

"You're a strong person," Alma said, as if reading my thoughts, "and struggle sometimes gives you powers you didn't know you had."

"It's certainly been true for you."

"It was true for me, but my parents died early, died of stress. When my mother went, I vowed I'd never forget where I came from, that I'd try to help young people like me, who were struggling to come up."

I envisioned the habitual lines of students outside Alma's door.

"But it isn't always easy working with your own group either," Alma said. "In *El Movimiento*, despite its talk about homeland and community, men were as slow as desert tortoises to share power with women. And even when Chicanas formed a separate group, there were internal quarrels and splits. I learned it's not just shared ethnicity that counts in alliances. It's politics and principles and heart."

★ ★ ★

At the entrance to the Deadly Planet, Alma and I took the outside elevator to the second floor. Sounds of conversation filtered into the hall, and as we entered the large, square conference room, already filled with people, we saw Isobel dressed in black with large turquoise earrings in the shape of long teardrops. It was not a look I could pull off, but it looked terrific on Isobel. We went up to give her an embrace.

"Thanks for coming."

"Wouldn't miss it," I said. As I looked around the room, I saw a lot of new faces but many that were familiar and dear to me as well. People from all over the university attended receptions like these, some to be polite but many to find a sense of communality that was often lacking in their own departments. Faculty of color, in particular, often felt alienated in their home departments that were otherwise all white. I took some salad and some red enchiladas with chicken, garlicky red pepper sauce, and tangy cotija cheese from the buffet table. They would be my dinner that evening. I poured some white wine into a plastic cup and sat on one of the chairs to eat. The red enchiladas were spicy and cheesy, really good. I looked at my colleagues forking through their food and drinking their wine. Even without talking to them, I felt connected, except perhaps to the new faculty member Alma had alluded to and who was bending now toward Alma's ear. Was she pitching some idea about her next advancement?

The room grew more crowded. The conversation level rose, and as I dropped my plate into the barrel for trash, I noticed a plump, middle-aged Chicana talking to Isobel. The woman's face had crumpled, and she seemed on the verge of tears. Isobel put her hand on her back, and the two disappeared out the door. When Isobel returned, she raised her long eyebrows at me from near the doorway. I went to her from across the room.

"I have something important I need to tell you." Isobel gave me one of her knowing looks. We entered the women's room across from the reception and checked the stalls for feet. We had the bathroom to ourselves.

"What's up?"

"I was just speaking with Yvonne Gonzalez, senior staff for Plant Biology. She did quite a bit of work for Peter Elliott." Isobel crossed her arms as if for emphasis. "He was double dipping."

"How do you mean?"

"He had two grants, one from the university and one from Syndicon and both were for the same work. He didn't report the Syndicon grant to the Conflict of Interest Committee that's supposed to oversee externally funded research. Syndicon had also given him some stock options, and I guess the idea was that they, and not the university, would have first dibs on patenting anything he discovered." Isobel's face took on that dark, cloudy look that I'd seen many times before. "He'd asked Yvonne to set up a private account for the money. Yvonne knew something was wrong, but she didn't dare say anything about it. You know in a budget crunch how they like to fire the staff. Yvonne has three kids and an aging mother, and she's the sole breadwinner."

"Wait a minute," I said, leaning against the frame of a yellow stall. "Peter ripped off the university and made Yvonne cover his tracks?" Isobel nodded so hard her earrings swayed back and forth like wind chimes.

"That's outrageous. And what an obscene way to treat your staff! We need to report him." I was amazed that Peter had engaged in such bold larceny, but perhaps it opened the door to a wider range of possibilities with regard to his poisoning. I hadn't a clue yet as to what those possibilities might be, but the revelation about the double dipping invited further thought.

"I want to figure out a way to protect Yvonne," Isobel said quickly. "Besides, Peter's in a coma. Let's let it rest for a bit."

★ ★ ★

At home after the reception, I had trouble getting down to work. I often felt at loose ends when Polly and Sadie were at Solomon's, unless, of course, I had to prepare a class, write a document, or think out an agenda for a meeting the next day, but tonight I was especially distracted and could think of little else but the Peter Elliott affair. It was as if a toxin had entered my own body. I tried to consider the different possibilities. If it had been a case of attempted harm or murder, was it my corn bread or someone else's that had been the vehicle?

And what had been the motive? Was it Save the Fields or someone else, perhaps someone I knew, who'd taken revenge on Peter for his research on GMOs and his ties to Syndicon? I didn't like to think about the latter prospect. Or maybe the poisoning was tied to Peter's double dipping. If someone knew about Peter's swindle, someone besides Yvonne—and I couldn't bring myself to suspect Yvonne—what would be the motive for trying to poison him? I wondered if someone else had been in on the double dipping and then tried to cover up their role.

I wasn't familiar with the world of scientific funding. As a professor in women's studies, I sometimes got fellowships that paid my salary for time off to write, but mainly I applied for, and received, small sums of research money, enough to pay a graduate student to check out books and compile bibliographies. There was nothing financial in women's studies, or in the humanities for that matter, to motivate a poisoning, not that I could see. But in the world of science? I wasn't sure. As I puzzled over the poisoning, I wandered about, looking in Polly's room, adjusting her green, jungle-themed bedspread, and stacking her papers neatly on her desk. I washed Sadie's water bowl and replaced the water, and finally put away the few dishes that had been drying in the wooden rack.

Then I froze at a sudden scuffling noise outside. What was that? I wondered, my body already taut. A raccoon again? After eleven years of marriage and only one of divorce, I was still unused to being in a house at night alone. While trying to fall asleep, I often lay in bed to the accompaniment of strange night noises. Delta winds rattled the windows, wild creatures of some sort thumped and scurried along the roof, and the house itself seemed to sigh and creak, while branches scraped uncannily along the outside walls. The occasional *woooh woooh* of a train only drew attention to my isolation. But tonight, my uneasiness over the poisoning, over the threats of violence against Tess and other colleagues, over the fact that I and people I cared about were suddenly suspects in some sort of crime made me jumpier than usual.

Seeking to distract myself, I headed to my computer. Earlier in the day, I'd e-mailed Tess to inquire about Peter, and now Tess had e-mailed back in her usual terse style: "Peter in coma. Pesticide in stomach. Police questioned wife. More later." Pesticide, how fitting for a campus that had once been devoted to agriculture. And, yes, of course, the wife! In cases of attempted murder, the spouse is always the first suspect. Peter's wife had a kitchen and plenty of opportunity and, from what I had learned about Peter's financial deceptions, his wife might have motivation as well.

Peter's duplicity in his work could very well have extended

to his personal life. A jealous wife might have sent corn bread in his lunch. I pictured Peter's wife as a gentle, modest-looking woman with several children. I felt sorry for her and wondered briefly if a woman like that would have gone so far as to poison her husband. But why not? As a professor of women's literature, I knew such things were not at all unknown. I remembered teaching Susan Glaspell's "A Jury of Her Peers," a story in which a meek, once cheerful, farm wife—Mrs. Wright, née Minnie Foster—is suspected of having strangled her sleeping, spirit-killing husband with a rope.

Two men, the sheriff and a neighbor named Mr. Hale, go to the crime scene to investigate. They're accompanied by their wives who've been charged with selecting items that Minnie might need while waiting for her trial. As the men search the upstairs bedroom and the barn, the wives find a clean apron for Minnie, notice that her canned fruit jars have exploded, and, in looking around her kitchen, see evidence of Minnie's distress and seeming guilt—a table half-wiped clean, a bag of sugar only partially poured into its wooden bucket, and a piece of quilting on which dainty sewing has suddenly given way to a batch of crude stitches. Women noticed things like that.

In Minnie's quilt bag they also find her pet canary, its neck broken, its body wrapped in silk and tucked into a box. It is obvious to the women that Mr. Wright has killed the canary, the one creature in the world that brought happiness to Minnie's diminished life. In a quiet act of sisterhood, the women decide against sharing this damning evidence with their husbands. It is the women, rather than the men, who have solved the crime, and it is the women who, as a jury of Minnie's peers, have found her undeserving of any punishment. The men, meanwhile, joke to each other about the women's interest in the details of Minnie's domestic life. "'Nothing here but kitchen things,'" the sheriff says, "with a little laugh for the insignificance of kitchen things." "'Would the women know a clue if they did come upon it?'" Mr. Hale asks with great jocularity. Geez. Even the meekest women could rebel against such treatment. But that was fiction. Did it happen in real life too? I knew it did.

As soon as my mind wandered back to the lab report, however, the consoling notion of a rebellious wife began to fade. What ingredients, other than poison, had the report found? Onions? Goat cheese? Was it my corn bread that had poisoned Peter Elliott or was it not? I resisted the idea that something I had baked with care and affection had become a vehicle for harm. I thought of *Like Water for Chocolate*, a Mexican romance I was about to teach. Food cooked with love prompted characters in the novel to feel amorous. But when the heroine's tears fell into the sister's wedding cake—her sister was marrying a man whom the heroine adored—those who ate the confection developed such longing for their own lost amours that they began crying, and then vomiting, everywhere. Although I had not been sad or angry when I made the corn bread, when I went to bed that night I dreamed I had prepared a large dish of enchiladas for a Haven Hall reception. Everyone who tasted them began to sicken—and then to die—until the floor was piled with bodies.

Red Enchiladas

Makes 12 enchiladas

4 guajillo peppers, seeds
removed
4 ancho peppers, seeds
removed
2 garlic cloves chopped
¼ teaspoon Mexican
oregano
Salt and pepper to taste
12 corn tortillas

⅓ cup of vegetable oil
2 cups of precooked and
shredded beef, pork, or
chicken
1½ cups of queso fresco,
crumbled
½ cup of white onion,
finely chopped

Optional Garnishes:

2 cups of precooked diced
potatoes and 2 cups of
precooked diced carrots

Finely shredded lettuce or
cabbage and radishes

Preheat oven to 350°F. (This is to keep the enchiladas warm as you finish assembling them.)

Slightly roast the peppers in a hot griddle, pressing them flat with the help of a spatula. Make sure not to burn them. This step takes a few seconds on each side of the peppers.

Once they are roasted, place them in a saucepan with water and turn the heat to medium and simmer for about 15 minutes or until they look soft.

Remove the saucepan from the stove and let chilies cool for

another 10–15 minutes. The pepper skins should look soft.

After the resting period, drain the peppers and place in the blender along with the garlic cloves. Add ½ cup of water and blend until you have a smooth sauce. If necessary, strain the sauce into a large bowl using a fine strainer. Season with the oregano, salt, and pepper, and set aside.

Add 2 tablespoons of vegetable oil in a large frying comal pan or skillet at medium heat. Add oil little by little as needed. Too much oil will produce a soggy tortilla.

Dip the tortilla into the sauce to lightly coat each side.

Place it in the skillet and briefly fry it a few seconds on both sides. Repeat with all the tortillas, adding more vegetable oil to the skillet as needed. Place fried tortillas in a dish while you make the rest and keep them warm in the oven.

To assemble the enchiladas, first place the meat filling in the center of the tortilla and fold or roll it.

Sprinkle the enchiladas with the cheese and onion.

If you decide to add the potatoes and carrots as garnish, peel the potatoes and carrots, cut in cubes, and boil until almost tender but still firm. Then drain and cool.

Use the same frying pan in which you fried the enchiladas to lightly fry the potatoes and carrots, adding a little more oil. The potatoes and carrots will be coated with some of the sauce sticking to the frying pan. Season with salt.

Garnish the enchiladas with potatoes and carrots, cheese, and optional lettuce and radishes.

You can play around with the amount of peppers, using more ancho peppers than guajillo or even making the sauce using just one of the peppers in the recipe, until you find the taste that you and your family enjoy best.

The sauce can be made one or two days ahead and also can be frozen for up to 2 months.

Adapted by permission of Mely Martinez at Mexico in My Kitchen
http://www.mexicoinmykitchen.com/2013/05/red-enchiladas-sauce-recipereceta.html

Chapter 5

Isobel paced back and forth in my living room in front of the burning fire as she read her draft of the resolution we'd agreed to at our meeting the week before. The women's, American, and ethnic studies programs were proposing to become a separate division with our own dean. Rather than disappearing into English or Sociology, we would continue to operate as independent programs, but, being united, we'd have more influence on campus, and a dean of our own would presumably understand and champion our work.

"They aren't going to go for this," the director of African American Studies said. He was given to pessimism, which while frustrating at times, I also knew to be well earned.

"Let's have a fallback position, then, a bottom line." Alma darted her dark eyes around the room. She sometimes found her colleagues less daring than she'd have liked. "If we can't become a separate division, let's say we want to be a named unit within the Division of Humanities. That way we won't be in competition with each other and the administration won't be able to play us off each other the way they like to do." Alma took some corn chips and laid them on her plate like exclamation marks. The director of American Studies put even more on his.

We were meeting at my home, and I'd served us homemade corn chips and guacamole. The chips were thick, salty, smelling freshly of corn—much more of a mouthful than chips from a bag. But for the first time in my life I'd paused before serving my guests food. Although the police had yet to announce that corn bread had been the vehicle for Peter's poisoning, informal news of my baking had spread across the Haven Hall community in just seven days. I wondered how long it would take before colleagues I didn't know so well started looking at me funny. Just the other day, indeed, the chair of the English Department had turned his basset-hound eyes in my direction and had given me an assessing look. Had he been considering me as a future, and potentially disruptive, member of his fiefdom? Had my hair been unusually limp and frizzy that afternoon? Or was he trying to decide if I was skilled in the art of poisoning? It was impossible to tell.

Even Alma had joked. "I'm eating these chips to show my faith in Emily and because they're really good."

I'd given her a grateful glance. But there'd been no time to discuss the Peter Elliott affair. The business at hand had been too pressing.

Isobel revised and then reread the document while standing at one side of the fireplace, where a blaze leapt invitingly. The temperature that day had climbed to eighty-six degrees, but the breeze from the local waterways had cooled the evening air, making a fire an appealing possibility. I liked the way fire drew a group together around its warmth, evoking ancestral memories of a distant time when heat, light, and community were necessary for survival, for protection, for keeping the dark at bay. The fire, like the food, seemed to give us all a feeling of confidence and connection, deepening our sense of common cause.

Our dismal meeting with Lorna, only one week ago, had brought us closer to each other, and, now, our programs were formally resisting the higher administration, defying its threats to cut our funding or fold our programs into giant departments where we would dissipate and dissolve. How would the guys at the top respond to our petition? Or, more to the point, what would they have Vice Provost Lorna Vogle do? Life was going to get interesting, or perhaps interesting was not the word.

★ ★ ★

The next morning I was eager to talk with Helena White, one of my closest friends in Women's Studies and a professor in the Department of Textiles. We had plans to take a walk together and then attend a meeting of women who were trying to improve conditions for females in the sciences on campus. Our ties to Women's Studies made such collaborations a matter of course, and being in Textiles, which was located in the College of Agriculture, brought Helena into regular contact with women scientists.

Taking a shortcut on my way to Textiles, I walked through the plaza in front of the Language Building—a looming nine-story pillar of precast concrete with a long tube of greenish glass attached to its front side. Why did so many of the buildings on campus look like science experiments? As I passed one of the benches in the courtyard, where a pair of students sat idly chatting, I noticed a copy of the *Arborville Courier* and saw its headline: POLICE SEEK UNKNOWN MAN. A man with a full beard and unruly hair, dressed in long brown pants and a faded red sweatshirt, was wanted for questioning. A witness had placed him near the Hog Barn in the early morning of October 11 when Peter Elliott was found. Long hair and a beard? Was he one of the vandals who had trampled the cornfields only weeks before? I realized that I didn't know what participants in Save the Fields looked like—and neither did anyone else. They worked at night and then, seemingly without a trace, they disappeared. And at any rate, why would long hair and a beard signify vandal, especially on a college campus? I wondered if Save the Fields was even involved in Peter's poisoning.

The note they'd left had hinted at physical harm, but would they have used corn bread—corn bread, really?—to achieve it? Talk about a strange and unwieldy weapon. I tried to imagine how they would have gotten Peter Elliott to eat it.

The idea seemed ridiculous, and yet Peter was so well funded by Syndicon and was so openly invested in corporate ownership of GMOs that it would make perfect sense for him to have been an object of Save the Field's wrath. I hadn't liked what I'd heard from Peter on the panel in the spring, but an attempted murder of someone for his point of view was threatening to everyone on campus. It soiled the air we all breathed like fumes from some torrent of oil gushing and spraying out of a broken pipe. And now I was a suspect in the case, and my act of sharing food had drawn suspicion not only to myself but to a whole group of colleagues with whom I was close.

And there was more to consider. Both Frank and I were persons of interest in the case, which hardly put our programs in a favorable light. Maybe our status as suspects would make Lorna feel even more justified in cutting our programs' funding or merging us into departments where we would quietly fade into the night. I remembered my nightmare about the poisoned enchiladas and my colleagues' deaths. I had responsibilities not just to myself and Women's Studies but to my ethnic studies colleagues and their programs as well. I had to find out all I could about the attempted poisoning. My head was a hive of speculation about vandals, wives, and poisoned corn bread as I headed toward Helena's office.

★ ★ ★

"Emily." Helena smiled her widest smile as she opened her office door. Helena, who wrote on the cultural meanings of fashion, was wearing a smart black dress that she'd purchased while attending a fashion conference in Eastern Europe

"Are you ready?" I looked forward to these walks with

Helena. They were islands of pleasure in what often felt like a choppy sea of struggle.

"Yes." Helena picked up a red leather bag. "The arboretum?"

The arboretum was the university's botanical garden, which followed Indian Creek, a sometimes clear and sometimes muddy stream that meandered through the southern edge of campus. Paths on both sides of the creek cut through well-tended borders of native trees and bushes and, at one point, through hilly swaths of closely trimmed lawns. Helena and I were fond of walking there. As we strolled down the shaded walk that led to the administration building, I filled Helena in about the nightmare, my worries, and details about the case that she hadn't heard of yet.

"Do you know Peter Elliott?" I asked.

"Oh yes." Helena's round, blue eyes widened. "He's kind of a legend."

"How so?"

"He's a man of appetites. He knows what he wants and usually gets it. He's done important work on corn that's doubly resistant to pests and disease in some way, and he's always well funded." We'd reached the administration building, but instead of entering we turned left and walked along a woodsy trail to its left side.

"Peter likes to think of himself as a gourmet. He eats a lot and drinks the best wines. But he dominates people and has a bad temper, and there's always talk about his being sexually involved with some of his students. Nothing proven as far as I know but he has a bad rep." Helena brushed at a vagrant strand of her corn silk hair, as if pushing the distasteful thought away.

Great, I thought, just great. The number of Peter's potential victims and, therefore, enemies had just multiplied.

"There was a young woman at the Hog Barn," I said, "when Peter was discovered. It seems she was really upset, more than most students would be about someone they only worked for."

I glanced at the overarching trees sheltering the path. Arbor State really was full of arbors. "I wondered about it. Maybe she was connected to him in some amorous way."

"How did you know there was a woman at the Hog Barn?"

"I met someone new in math. He's the one who found Peter that morning."

"What was *he* doing there?"

"Taking photographs. He has an office at the Institute of Analytical Dynamics right next door."

"This is new." Helena gave me a sly, inquiring look. "What's he like?"

"Smart, polite, good looking in an understated way. All we've done is have coffee. But I can tell you more after our date. We're doing dinner and a movie tomorrow night." I looked forward to having more to share. Ever warm and supportive, Helena made a congenial confidante.

On the other side of the administration building, we passed through a wooden arbor draped in ivy and then walked down a grassy hill that led to a place where the creek formed a modest lake. There was a puddle in the middle of the lawn and a half dozen mallard ducks were gathered there drinking. Three ducks with iridescent green heads waddled up to us quacking for food. They were used to being fed, although it wasn't good for them and posted signs warned visitors not to feed the wildlife. Both Helena and I laughed.

"No, we're not going to feed you," Helena said. The sun glanced off the water, some ducks swimming in the lake left quiet ripples behind them, and knots of staff sat on benches quietly eating lunch. "I love the arboretum. There's a sense of harmony here."

"Someone's given it a lot of thought." I stooped to read a sign that identified a wild-looking pink rose bush at the water's edge. I liked how the signs gave plants a kind of dignity, inviting passersby to pause and take them in.

Near the last bridge the arboretum path diverged, one part leading over the bridge past a gazebo to the other side of the creek, the other disappearing into a grove of redwoods. I saw a flicker of reddish shirt and bushy hair at a distance among the giant trees. A man in brown pants and a red sweatshirt was walking rapidly down the path in the opposite direction. I stopped and put a hand on Helena's arm.

"Stop. Did you see that man?"

"No, where?"

"Over there on the redwood path." I pointed. "He's gone. He looked like the man the police are searching for."

"I saw that story. Who do you think it could be?"

"He looked homeless, kind of wild and unkempt. I wondered earlier if he were one of the vandals, though maybe that doesn't make sense."

"Could Save the Fields be walking around campus?" Helena studied the redwood path nervously. "I hadn't thought of that."

I remembered the sense of shock that had torn through the College of Agriculture like a flash of lightning after the crops were ruined. Helena had felt it deeply.

"They did leave a threatening note, and Tess Ryan was followed home the night before Peter was found. She's usually unflappable, but it really unsettled her."

"It makes me so angry. Where does vandalism get us? And they tore up the wrong field at that and just at harvest. Now the graduate student who planted that cornfield has to start her project all over again. The damage they did cost her a year of work."

We walked gingerly to the edge of the redwoods and peered down the path. There was no sight of the man.

"Let's go down the path the other way," Helena suggested, hugging herself as if staving off a shiver. We retraced our steps and headed west along the arboretum path until we reached two towering palm trees, some enormous yuccas, and a prickly pear cactus where white cabbage butterflies flickered in the sun, landed briefly on some bladderpod bushes, and then fluttered again, always in motion. It was a peaceful contrast to our unsettled state at the redwoods only minutes before, peaceful that is, until, between the cactus and the yuccas, an opening in the bushes brought something else disturbing into view.

"Look at the water tower," I said. "It makes me queasy just to be near it, but I can't help staring." The tower—a huge white metal dome with the name Arbor State painted on its side—sat astride four giant metal legs that were interlocked with a web of sturdy braces. At fifteen stories high, it was the tallest structure on campus and a well-known landmark of the university. I studied the tower now with morbid fascination. I was terrified of heights, but was always drawn to looking at whatever made me dizzy.

A narrow white ladder hung on one of the tower's back legs, and at the very top of the ladder a fenced-in catwalk skirted the gigantic cake-shaped dome. I imagined standing on that catwalk, looking down, experiencing that sense of tingling dread that high places always induced in me. I stared at the tower intently for a moment, becoming a little faint. I hated the way it loomed over me, how—like the sudden appearance of the man in red—it disrupted the peacefulness of the walk, making me feel that Arbor State was not so sheltered a place as I liked to imagine it. Helena and I continued our progress, and I was relieved when the water tower passed out of view.

"Should we turn back now?" I asked.

"Perhaps we'd better."

It was time for the meeting with women scientists.

★ ★ ★

Women wearing plain-looking shirts and khakis, clearly scientific types, were filing into a classroom in the white-columned building devoted to chemistry. I saw the flame of Tess's hair and Helena and I moved toward her.

"Any news about Peter?" I asked.

"I heard they questioned Juan Carlos Vega in Environmental Toxicology." Tess grimaced.

I remembered him from the GMO panel last spring, the young half-Chicano, half-Native American professor with a fine long nose and a black braid down the middle of his back. He'd been vehement about GMOs and had warned about the possibility that the modified seeds might migrate into Mexico and contaminate traditional Mexican crops.

"Corn is our identity," he'd said with passion, looking directly at Peter Elliott.

Peter had merely stroked his skimpy mustache, his face impassive. Juan Carlos, too, had attended the reception with the corn bread. I hadn't talked to him, but I remembered seeing his braid from across the room. Now it occurred to me that Juan Carlos had had access to the corn bread and, as a professor in Environmental Toxicology, to pesticides as well and that his department's offices were in Bauman Hall not far from Animal Science where the reception had been held.

I wondered if the police knew that. Frank might have told them about the reception, but had they known about the GMO panel and about Juan Carlos's anger? Frank, of course, could have told the police about that too, but I doubted Frank would have exposed a friend of the program to suspicion. Maybe someone else had told the police about the tensions that day. I strained to remember who'd been in the audience. A lot of people, unfortunately, whom I didn't know.

The meeting for women scientists began, and Tess, Helena, and I scrambled for some seats.

"Good morning," the speaker said. A professor in Physiology, and a woman I trusted, Katherine Breyer had a scientist's rationality but was emotionally engaged with women's interests and clearly opposed to the less-than-democratic elements of a university that increasingly privileged scientific competition while giving women in science less support than men. She herself had once served as vice provost, and I'd sometimes sought her advice about how to respond to unfriendly moves against Women's Studies.

"Let me bring you up to date. We've agreed that we will begin our grant-writing project by gathering data about inequities for women in science on campus." Katherine was a solid woman with gray hair and large tortoiseshell glasses, which gave her a rather owl-like presence. "We're proposing to obtain the number and percentage of women faculty in science, the percentage of women scientists with tenured positions by rank and department, and we'll also collect data on tenure and promotion outcomes for women and men." Heads around me nodded with approval and support. The women scientists, hearing talk of data, were in their element.

"As you know all too well," Katherine continued, peering at us over her glasses, "a recent report has revealed that while women in math, physical sciences, and engineering constitute 12.4 percent of the hiring pool for tenured faculty, women are only 7.8 percent of tenured faculty in science on campus and only 7 percent of the hires. Other inequities in pay, promotion, and lab space have also been uncovered."

I wondered how Tess's lab space compared to Peter's and what the relative speed of their promotions had been. A young woman with a face pale as an egg, a graduate student I supposed because of her youth, was taking copious notes.

"We'll also count the women in endowed chairs, but to emphasize the positive we'll compile lists of the departments that have been successful in hiring women and we'll lay out what they did to make that possible."

I admired Katherine's broad grasp of the situation for women scientists and the psychology of stressing the positive when one could. Plans to improve the fortunes of women on campus always stirred my blood, and working with others gave me a sense of hope, which was sometimes hard to come by. The university's growing emphasis on consolidating power and privilege at the top—part of its incipient immersion in corporate practices and points of view—only made women's historically unequal situation worse.

"We've also agreed to evaluate the cost to women of trying to combine family and careers," Katherine continued. "We'll eventually develop a plan for on-campus childcare, so more women will want to come here and stay. We'll be saying that supporting childcare is as important as supporting high-risk research."

I wasn't sure what "high risk" research was. My degree was in literature, after all, though writing about gender had not been without its hazards early on in my career. Even at Arbor State, the chair of English, or so I'd heard, had described my work as "sociology." Trained in literary criticism, I'd been pleased at the idea of having a sociologist's skills as well, although the chair of English hadn't used the word as a compliment, more as an allusion to my assumed alignment with the Prince of Darkness.

As the speaker continued, a low click told me that someone was entering the seminar room. I looked back to see Vice Provost Vogle dart through the door, wearing a bright baby blue suit. I had to give her credit. That suit was a spark of life among the pale shirts and khakis—like a blue bird or like the sky outside now that it was October. Lorna tilted her head as if trying to get a better view of her surroundings. She had at least shown up, but I wondered if it were out of genuine interest and concern or just for show.

The pale young woman raised her hand. She could have been attractive, but her pinched-up face looked dour, and she wore the drabbest outfit in the room—a navy polo shirt and beat-up jeans.

"I'm Jenny Archer of Plant Biology. Are we going to address

the welfare of graduate students? Because there are a lot of things I could say about that."

"Yes, we do want to address graduate student issues," Katherine said.

"She's one of Peter's students," Tess whispered to me. "He's her major professor."

"I'm tired of professors getting us to work on their topics and do their work for them and then not giving us proper credit on the papers they publish. To get jobs, we need publications that have our own names on them."

More greed on Peter's part, I thought. He was sounding worse and worse.

"We need more oversight, someone we can go to, someone who will listen and who can exert some power."

A recent survey had revealed that female graduate students in general wanted better mentoring and that they preferred women. Women gave more of their time and attention, understood them, and listened to issues about combining family and career. I assumed that women professors in science were also less likely to publish their students' work without giving them credit, though whether this was true or not, I wasn't certain. I'd also heard a number of women graduate students express serious doubts about pursuing a life in science, despite the attraction of its flexible hours and exciting new discoveries, because they desperately wanted families as well as careers and were daunted by how hard women faculty in science had to work.

"We don't want to follow your model," one young woman had said pointedly at a women-in-science talk last year.

It wasn't hard to understand. The culture of science in the university had taken shape when most men had stay-at-home wives to take care of children and their other domestic needs. Now, women in science were a growing part of the work force, but no provisions had been made to reflect that shift. Tess was lucky—she had a husband who shared childcare and household labor. Many women did not. The competitive nature of work in the sciences, the lack of provision for child-rearing, which women still took care of by and large, and women's uneven access to resources made for a workload that was hard to bear. I wondered for a fleeting moment what Wilmer's arrangements with his wives had been.

I felt sorry for Jenny Archer, who was angry and looked distressed, and now her major professor was in a coma. That couldn't be good. At the same time, I wondered what Jenny's relation to Peter had been. I hoped she was not one of those with whom Peter, according to rumor, had gone too far. At the conclusion of the meeting, I approached Tess once again.

"Listen, Tess, do you think the police know that Juan Carlos confronted Peter at the GMO panel? I don't think Frank would have told the police that."

"I don't know," Tess said. "But if they're questioning people who disagreed with Peter, I must be next."

Baked Tortilla Chips

1 12-ounce package corn
  tortillas
1 tablespoon vegetable oil
3 tablespoons lime juice

1 teaspoon ground cumin
1 teaspoon chili powder
1 teaspoon salt

Preheat oven to 350°F

Cut each tortilla into 8 chip-sized wedges and arrange the wedges in a single layer on a cookie sheet.

In a mister, combine the oil and lime juice. Mix well and spray each tortilla wedge until slightly moist.

Combine the cumin, chili powder, and salt in a small bowl and sprinkle on the chips.

Bake for about 7 minutes. Rotate the pan and bake for another 8 minutes or until the chips are crisp, but not too brown. Serve with salsas, garnishes, or guacamole.

Recipe provided by www.Allrecipes.com.
Recipe submitted by Michele O'Sullivan.

Chapter 6

I gazed through the French doors to the swimming pool outside. It was mainly for Polly, who was a dedicated swimmer, but
I also liked to look at it, as if it were a private lake or a reflecting
pond. It helped distract me from the fact that most of my life
took place in my study and my office, in the offices of other
people, in classrooms, and in meeting rooms all over campus.
Today, however, I was eager to sit at my desk and turn on my
computer. After yesterday's information about Juan Carlos Vega,
I wanted to explore the website of Environmental Toxicology.
The situation of the toxicology professor Juan Carlos Vega was
not promising. He'd been at the reception, had had access to
my corn bread and to poison, and had publically confronted
Peter. I didn't want to think him guilty, a man with ties to my
colleagues in Native American and Chicana/o Studies, but I
was worried and curious nonetheless. If I could talk with him,
maybe I could put my mind at rest, and since we both were
suspects in the case, perhaps, together, we could think of clues.
I wanted to find his office hours and pay him a visit.

I'd had little contact with Juan Carlos at the GMO panel in
the spring, but in a brief conversation with him after the pro-
ceedings, I'd learned that we'd both grown up in Compton, just
below South Central Los Angeles. Long ago, the region had
been horse fields, but after World War II, pastures and farms had
given way to tracts of houses and to factories, and Compton

had supported modest families like my own for many years. For most of my childhood, I'd thought of Compton as just an ugly town, its main boulevard displaying so many glinting car lots that it was hard to tell where one began and the other one ended. I recalled the dried fields, the aging oil rigs, and the acrid smell of petrol that I'd been driven through on the way to my favorite beach.

Years later, someone had written an essay about the city which I'd read and underlined out of fascination with a past I'd lived through but hadn't understood. I'd learned that when I was a child, forty-five thousand people had lived in Compton, only fifty of whom were black. A settlement of Mexican Americans had been confined to the north of the city in a barrio I'd never seen. But after the Supreme Court had overturned race covenants barring nonwhites from the city's center, middle-class blacks and Latinos had begun moving into town. Racial tension and violence had exploded.

Until high school I had little sense of these tensions. My family had lived in an all-white neighborhood, and I'd attended all-white schools. It was only in high school, which was at least formally integrated, that I had come to some sense of social injustice and to an understanding that people on the margins could act together on their own behalf. Now, I found myself wondering what Juan Carlos's experience of Compton High had been. I tried to imagine him, tall and rangy as a colt, with a mane of dark hair, walking down its crowded hallways some fifteen years after I myself had been there.

As I scanned the website for more information about Juan Carlos, I was intrigued to see that a Teresa Fuentes-Elliott, an associate professor of Environmental Toxicology, who studied pesticide residues on fruits, vegetables, and coffee, was one of Juan Carlos's colleagues. Could Teresa Fuentes-Elliott be married to Peter? In her picture on the website, Teresa looked nothing like the plain, long-suffering woman whom I had so

confidently imagined Peter's wife to be. Teresa was pretty with
thick brown eyebrows, a larger-than-life smile, and long, wavy,
caramel-colored hair. She'd come from Colombia, and she
looked young, much younger than Peter. I wondered if Teresa
had met Peter as a student herself. If so, Peter's reputation for
womanizing might not surprise her. Was she used to it? Or,
as I now began to speculate, did she lead an independent life
as I had tried to do with Solomon? I remembered thinking
how wives were always the first suspects. Would a young, independent, and pretty woman be more or less likely to have fed
poisoned corn bread to a cheating husband than the modest
homemaker I had first fancied her to be? I wasn't sure, but
I resolved to ask Juan Carlos whether Teresa was married to
Peter, and, if so, how she was taking her husband's illness.

★ ★ ★

Juan Carlos's door was open for office hours when I arrived in
the Department of Environmental Toxicology in Bauman Hall.
I knocked on the door frame and stuck my head inside. Juan
Carlos sat at a desk, which faced the door and was dominated
by a large computer. To the right some black metal bookcases
were stuffed with books and many teetering stacks of paper.

"Juan Carlos, I'm Emily Addams. I don't know whether
you remember me or not. We spoke briefly after the panel on
GMOs last spring. We both grew up in Compton."

"Oh, yes, Emily, I remember," he said, standing up. "Come
in, please, and have a seat."

He smiled. His even white teeth stood out against his tan
skin. He's very good-looking, I thought. I had a weakness for
men wearing long, black braids. We shook hands and I sat in
the chair next to his desk.

"Let's see, you came to Compton in the eighties, after I'd
already left. Were the used car lots still there on the boulevard?"

"Oh yes, they were still there."

"And did you go to the beach through the oil fields?"

"I didn't go to the beach much, but I remember the fields and the rigs. Things were getting rough in Compton by the time we came, but we lived in Richland Farms, a rural part of Compton out near the airport. My dad raised horses and we farmed a little. It was a different life from what went on in the rest of the city. There's a picture of my family." He gestured toward the bookcase. I could see a picture of a mother, four children, and a father wearing a cowboy hat. Horses in the field behind them had stretched brown necks to graze.

"I've never heard of Richland Farms. All I think of when I imagine Compton are rows of shiny cars. I think you told me you were born in Mexico?"

"We crossed over when I was ten from Michoacán where my family ran a farm. After we came to California, my parents picked grapes for a time in the Central Valley, but they began to get sick from working in the fields—headaches, nausea, vomiting. My father's vision started to go. People didn't care what they did to farm workers." Furrows appeared between his dark brows.

"What did they get sick from?"

"Furadan. It's a liquid pesticide you spray on crops." Juan Carlos paused. "It's one of the reasons I went into toxicology."

"Is it something you work on?"

"I've studied it. But I'm more interested in developing pesticides that don't make people sick." Juan Carlos tilted his head as if my presence had begun to puzzle him.

"Juan Carlos, I've come to you because I think it was my corn bread they found in Peter Elliott's hand the day he was poisoned. The police questioned me and even searched my kitchen, and I think they already knew I was the one who'd made it, though I don't know how. I understand they came to talk to you as well. I left the reception before you did. Did you notice anyone carrying the bread away?"

The muscles in Juan Carlos's jaw tightened.

"No, the police already asked me that. Look, Peter Elliott is a corporate pig, though that's an insult to pigs. He basically works for Syndicon, and he's effectively a lobbyist. There are a lot of people on campus who dislike what he stands for." Juan Carlos pushed up the sleeves of his blue cotton shirt. "Syndicon owns ninety percent of the world's market in GMOs. They take native seeds, modify them, and then patent the seeds and technologies. If a farmer is caught growing their corn, even if the corn seeds have drifted into his field from somewhere else, they sue the farmer."

"I know. It's outrageous!" It really was outrageous. I'd learned about it for the first time on the panel last spring.

"And then there's the whole issue of pollution." Juan Carlos raised his hands in the air. "Some of their corn is used to create inedible products. What if that corn drifts into a farmer's field of edible corn? And there's the matter of culture as well. Many Mexicans see corn as sacred, as the origin of life. Some indigenous people believe that humans were born from maize, and our seeds go back ten thousand years. To endanger those seeds is an aggression against our culture, our deeply held beliefs, our very identity, and it's a threat to plant diversity in general, which is necessary for sustaining life."

Juan Carlos's bark-brown eyes held mine steadily. How had Peter managed to ignore a gaze like that?

"But Syndicon cares nothing about that. Profit is everything. The rest of the world be damned." Juan Carlos let his hands rest on the desk once more. "Big farmers put profit before the health of their workers, and big corporations elevate profit over everyone and everything in the world, and now, throughout the whole country, some university scientists who are supposed to make public service come first are almost paid employees of corporations." Juan Carlos paused, stretched his fingers flat on the desk, and looked at me sadly. "I'm sorry to go on like this."

"It makes me angry too." I thought briefly about Lorna's lack of concern for those she saw as lower forms of life. Lorna, despite her bright scarves and perky suits, was beginning to remind me of Peter. "I hope that Peter's not the future. Do you think he is?"

"I hope not, but nationally it's the way research is going. Look, if this is why you've come—to find out whether I poisoned Peter—poisoning Peter would not go far in changing the new system. Besides, given my work in toxicology, would I be stupid enough to poison someone? Not to mention that I don't believe in harming other human beings."

Oh no, I thought. I've put my foot in it.

"No, that's not why I came. Frank wouldn't have poisoned anyone either. I just thought if we could put our heads together, think of who might have wanted to kill Peter, how it might have been done, we could protect other people who might be in harm's way—who knows if this will be an isolated incident. And we could get our own names cleared. Both of us are suspects along with Frank." I fell silent for a moment and glanced at the family photo once more. "I noticed that a Teresa Fuentes-Elliott is a colleague of yours. Is she married to Peter?"

Juan Carlos blushed, and then, appearing not to hesitate, said yes.

"How's she taking all this?

"I hear she's doing all right. She's on leave this quarter, so we don't see her often. But I've heard she's taking it well. Apparently, she's at the hospital a lot."

"Well, thanks for talking with me." I'd made Juan Carlos uncomfortable and was eager to be off. But I'd learned something that might be important in the future. There was more than collegiality between Juan Carlos and Teresa.

* * *

I stood before my bathroom mirror. Wilmer and I were going on our first real date, but there was barely enough time to get ready. I'd spent more time researching, and then visiting with, Juan Carlos than I'd intended. All I could do was put on more makeup. My eyes were my one good feature, and I liked to play them up. I relined them, applied more lipstick, powdered my nose, and sighed at my hair. It hung straight again. I'd curled it with an iron that morning as usual, but the curl, as always, hadn't lasted. My hair was straight and fine, and my hairdresser assured me that every hairdo I admired was beyond its meager capacity. Miriam had had long thick hair before the brain tumor and for a long time after. How I had envied it, so lush and so obedient at every length and in every style.

Tonight, I would wear the long black jacket, the bronze long skirt, and the white T-shirt that I'd worn to see Juan Carlos. No time to change, but I added turquoise earrings. On cue my eyes picked up the color. Okay, I have one gift, I thought. Best be thankful for that.

"I thought we'd do Chinese," Wilmer said when he arrived.

Was it my imagination or did he linger a bit at my eyes?

"There's a place I really like in Valley Town and then we can see the movie we talked about, *The Sixth Sense*. I found a theater where it's still playing."

"Sounds good."

"Any more developments in the Peter Elliott affair?" Wilmer asked as we began to drive east.

"Several." I filled him in about my own questioning, about the police search of my kitchen, about Frank, Juan Carlos, Teresa, and the man in red. We were passing the rice fields on the side of the freeway, which served as a wildlife sanctuary, when I saw a flash of snow. An egret had taken sudden flight. "And then there's the young woman you encountered. I've thought about her reaction. She must have had some personal connection with Peter to be that upset. I've learned that he has a reputation for being sexually involved with some of his students."

"I wondered about that myself. She called him 'Peter' at first, but when I asked her who he was, she said 'Professor Elliott.' And she was crying as if her heart had been broken."

"Yes, there must be something between them." I found Wilmer's analytical turn of mind much to my liking. He was willing to apply it to human relations and everyday affairs, things that I cared about and that the poisoning and my own status as suspect had made of crucial importance.

"Tell me in more detail about what happened that morning."

"I'd gotten up early to photograph the hog barn." Wilmer glanced at me with a tentative smile. "I like to take pictures of rural things—barns, old houses, fences. My grandfather taught me photography, though he never let me touch his expensive cameras. He was a tough old bird, a farmer."

"Where'd you grow up?"

"Arkansas."

"Ah, go on." I was right about his country-like appearance.

"I was looking at the barn, kind of moving in and then moving away and it occurred to me that I could get the Hog Barn and the Institute together, you know, lining up two symbols—one of the future, one of the past. I was feeling excited like I do sometimes when I'm breaking through in math, so I walked to the north corner of the barn, stood in front of a corridor that ran between the pens, and put the camera to my eye to compose the shot . . ."

"And?"

"I aimed too low and got the pigs. One was snuffling at something in the mud, so I lowered the camera and focused on a spot just beyond its head." Wilmer paused for emphasis. "It was the body of a man lying in the mud."

"Oh." What would I have done if I'd stumbled on a body just where I'd least have thought to find one?

"What'd you do next?"

"I kind of froze for a minute. It's not something you'd expect to see. Then I climbed the rails, jumped into the corridor, and ran to what I now know to be Peter Elliott."

"What'd he look like?" I'd heard that line on a television crime show.

"He was lying on his stomach, half his face in the muck, one hand next to his body, the other one stretched above his head. I remember thinking that he looked like he was reaching for something."

Reaching for something? That certainly fit with what I've heard about Peter Elliott's ambitious nature.

"I turned him over." Wilmer shuddered faintly. "Half his face was covered with yellow vomit and dark brown sludge, and the front of his clothes was smeared with slime. He smelled terrible."

"What was he wearing?" I don't know why I asked that one, but I did.

"Khaki shorts, a navy polo shirt, expensive sneakers."

Of course, the Arborville warm weather uniform.

"So I called 911, wiped his face with my handkerchief, and started CPR. Thirty compressions, two breaths, and so on."

I surmised from this that Wilmer had been a Boy Scout in his youth. The idea was reassuring. Didn't Boy Scouts know how to take care of things in all sorts of risky situations?

"Did he wake up?"

"He coughed but didn't come to consciousness. And then I heard a high voice calling 'Peter.' It was the young woman intern."

"What'd *she* look like?"

"Chinese American, long black hair, very pretty. She had on a red shirt, jeans, and a pair of rubber boots."

I hadn't needed to ask. Wilmer had anticipated my interest in the young woman's clothing.

"When she saw Peter, she started crying like all get out. I asked her who he was and she told me Professor Elliott and I asked how she knew him."

"What'd she say?"

"That he was doing research on hog nutrition, that he was around a lot, and that she fed his hogs along with all the rest."

We'd left the freeway now and were entering the scruffy outskirts of Valley Town.

"That's it?" It seemed to me there was more to know about her circumstances, maybe a lot more than she'd let on. "What was she doing at the barn so early?"

"I asked her that. She said she lived upstairs in the barn and took care of the hogs and checked on them at night and that she was just coming out to feed the sows. And then she kneeled right next to him and looked hard at his face and cried even more. I couldn't offer her my handkerchief because it was covered in mud, but I did assure her that he was breathing, just not conscious."

That country gentleman thing again. I was liking it.

"Then what happened?"

"I wanted to ask more questions, but the ambulance arrived and I had to talk to the police. That's when I looked down at Peter and noticed something I hadn't seen before. The hand at his side was holding something yellow. It turned out to be a bit of corn bread."

The corn bread again. I wondered if the young woman at the hog yard was fond of baking. Maybe I could make a trip to the barn and find out. Wilmer and I continued on about the Peter Elliott case until we arrived at the restaurant and the warm smell of garlic and ginger wrapped us in a savory cloud.

The Golden Lotus was a surprisingly elegant place with brass poles, booths in red and bronze leather, round mirrors over the tables, and round portholes between the booths, etched with Chinese renderings of what looked like rabbits. White plates held napkins folded in a swan-like way. I loved booths, their softness, the way they sheltered, and I was impressed that Wilmer knew enough to take me to a place like this. It was beautiful and comforting. We ordered our meal, Kung Pao Chicken for Wilmer and Garlic Eggplant for me—I was excessively fond of eggplant—along with a side dish of Pine Nuts and Corn. If there was something with corn on the menu, I was bound by my research to taste it, and this was a dish I'd never had. After ordering, we both settled back with our wine and began to talk about our campus lives. The waiter soon appeared with our dishes.

"I won a prize in mathematics," Wilmer said, "so I should be getting a promotion this year."

"Wait, you get promoted for winning a prize?"

"Usually."

I put my chopsticks down on the plate. The corn and pine nuts had been sweet and crunchy.

"That would never happen in women's studies. You'd be lucky to get a congratulatory e-mail from the dean."

"Really?" Wilmer looked at me in surprise.

★ ★ ★

The movie proved to be a thriller in which a child psychologist does therapy with a boy who sees dead people walking around like regular people. I got edgy watching thrillers and movies about the supernatural, and this film was full of sudden, ghastly appearances of ghosts, some hanged, all hollow eyed, one reaching out—suddenly—from under a bed. Movies like these stayed with me long after I'd seen them. I knew that when I returned home I would turn on all the lights. I wished Wilmer would hold my hand. Given the scary film, it would have been soothing, but he made no move to do so. Was there some code of behavior among mathematicians I didn't understand? No touching on first dates, just talk about promotions?

Was there some absence of affect on Wilmer's part? Or did he just lack interest? After the movie we drove straight home.

"That was intense," I said, as we stood on my front porch to say goodnight. "I don't like it when there are surprises at the end. Why did the psychologist have to be a ghost as well? But I enjoyed it. I'm glad we went."

"I enjoyed it too. Thanks for coming. Well, good night."

He stood there for a moment, the front porch light glinting on his glasses, but he made no move to hug me or even shake my hand.

"Good night," I said at last. Wilmer turned and then ambled to his car. Odd, I thought as I turned my key in the door. Maybe he's not attracted to me. Yet our conversation had been lively.

I entered the living room, hung up my jacket, and parked my purse on the kitchen counter. Had I asked too many questions about his discovery of Peter Elliott? Had that been boring? Or, wait. Did Wilmer interpret my interest as some kind of sign that I myself had been involved in the crime? Could he possibly think that I was the one who'd poisoned Peter? I opened the refrigerator to look for wine and found an opened bottle. But Wilmer had been the one at the Hog Barn that morning, not me. And why had I been so trusting of him? He said he hadn't known who Peter was, but was he lying? I poured myself a full glass. No, he'd been too much of a gentleman, too open. He'd probably been a Boy Scout for God's sake. And he'd gotten Peter breathing again. Why poison someone if you're going to save him afterward? There was no real reason to doubt his word, though still . . .

I leaned against the white tile counter, took a long sip of the wine, and began to think once more about our talk at the restaurant. I'd been taken aback by the fact that mathematicians were promoted for winning prizes. Winning prizes did not bring you promotion in women's or ethnic studies or even in the humanities—that I knew for sure. And promotions in math were tied to short papers while my nonmathematical colleagues had to write long papers and publish books. One world, it would seem, was designed for quick advance. Another, for extended labor at lower pay.

Feeling a sudden need for comfort food, I opened a cupboard, found a package of Carr's Water Biscuits at the back, grabbed a few from the box, and began to eat. It irked me about the prizes being linked to promotions, just as it irked me that women, and especially women in ethnic studies, were always less advanced in their careers than their male peers. It wasn't a question of the men being better. It was that many women tended to things other than their publications and paid a price for it. I munched on a cracker, which proved, not surprisingly, to be stale and took another swig of wine to wash it down. Women in ethnic studies, in particular, spent large amounts of time with their students, organized conferences and lecture series, were frequently asked to sit on committees and direct their programs, and devoted a good deal of energy to building relationships.

Many of them tended to children and sometimes husbands at home as well. And even when they didn't do those things, they were promoted more slowly than men. I remembered the first cover of *Ms. Magazine*—a women with eight arms like those of the goddess Shiva, one holding a duster, another a frying pan, another a typewriter, another a phone, another a mirror. There was a baby inside the woman's womb and the woman was weeping. From overwork, I guessed. Still I'd rather be a woman—the wine by now was having a softening effect. I liked being trained to sensitivity and care—and I'd like to know more about Wilmer Crane.

Corn with Pine Nuts

Serves:1–2

½ green pepper	1 tablespoon olive oil
1 or 2 green onions	1½ cups frozen corn
⅓ cup pine nuts	½ teaspoon sea salt

Chop the green pepper and green onions, set aside. Lightly toast the pine nuts in the pan, stirring so as not to burn them. Set aside.

Heat the stainless steel frying pan for 1–2 minutes, lower the heat to medium, add 1 tablespoon olive oil, and then turn the pan and let the oil coat the pan.

Add green pepper and green onion. Fry for 2 minutes.

Add corn and continue to fry for 2 minutes. Add pine nuts and fry for 1 minute.

Turn off the heat and add the salt, mix well, and serve.

Note: raw corn kernels don't work well in this dish. If you want to use fresh corn, you will have to cook it for a bit first. Lightly steaming the corn or boiling it for a few minutes will work.

Adapted by permission of Annie Taylor Chen at VeganAnn http:// veganann.com/corn-with-pine-nuts/.

Chapter 7

The air was still cool, a perfect morning for strolling through the stalls of the farmer's market. Laid out in Arborville's Central Park, under a green metal shelter, the market's long rows of stands were piled with organic broccoli, lettuces, and apples; with golden honeys, spreads, and oils; with whole wheat croissants and long brown loaves of fresh French bread; with hunks of fragrant cheese; and with bouquets of yellow sunflowers and pink dahlias. There were organic Merlots and gluten-free brownies, not that I bought either one, but the bounty was pleasing. Flanking the market on the sidewalk to the north, card tables offered information about 4-H clubs, animal rights, ecological beekeeping, and the Arborville Peace Coalition. At the other end of the market, stalls devoted to arts and crafts displayed wind chimes, rustic birdhouses, and glass jewelry.

To enter the market was to feel life's richness, provided you were fairly middle-class, of course. I, being thoroughly middle-class by now, bought a latte for myself and a hot chocolate for Polly, and then we entered the market to browse. The stands were crowded with shoppers, and passage was slow. Outside, on the park's grassy open field, a trio of banjo players were setting up their chairs. Polly pulled me gently toward one of the bakeries offering chocolate croissants.

"Please, Mom."

"Okay." I usually tried to steer her away from sugary things, but she had the morning off from school because of a teacher training event, and the occasion seemed to call for a special treat. Getting out my wallet, I noticed a sign pointing out fresh corn bread.

"I'll have a chocolate croissant, please. What's in your corn bread?"

"There's one plain and one with peppers." The young woman at the stand had long flaxen hair like a figure in a fairy tale, the perfect woman to be selling healthy foods and not at all likely to have injected poison into corn bread.

"Do you ever make it with caramelized onions and goat cheese?"

"Gee, I don't think so. It sounds good though."

I was disappointed. The farmer's market was the one place in Arborville I'd seen corn bread being offered for sale. Where else could I look?

Polly, both hands full, gestured toward the pumpkins with her croissant. I laughed and followed her to the stand. I'd been uneasy the evening before, sleeping alone in the house, with hair-raising scenes from *The Sixth Sense* still fresh in my memory. Odd how heartening it was to have Polly and the dog with me at night, even though I was the adult and the human being—the one who'd have to take charge should anyone try to break in. Sadie might bark if she heard something in the middle of the night, but she welcomed all strangers, jumping on them, slapping her golden paws on their shoulders, happy to see them no matter who they might be. After my restless night, it felt especially good to have Polly at my side and to enter this community-based market, which ran, after all, on a sense of trust and goodwill.

The wholesomeness of Arborville was in its DNA. The place felt more like a fantasy of Small Town, USA, than a city with heated politics and a long history of debates about whether houses should or should not be built on the surrounding fields. In March, the farmer's market celebrated National Pig Day, which featured pig costumes, swine-related crafts, hog-shaped rolls from a local bakery, a piglet petting zoo, and, strangely perhaps, bacon. Children, being children, even in Arborville, had to be strictly forbidden from pulling the piglets' tails or shaking them awake. On the Fourth of July, Arborville held festivities during the day and set off fireworks in the city park at night. People spread out picnics on their blankets, and children ran free. On Halloween, children in costumes, along with their parents, visited Arborville's downtown businesses, where the children were handed candy by owners who themselves were often dressed as pirates or ballerinas. In December a lighted holiday parade featured antique tractors and motorcycles, floats, horses, and Santa and Mrs. Claus. Arborville seemed a benign place to raise a child—though here, as everywhere, some were eager to make profits at the community's expense.

Halloween was getting close, so I followed Polly to the pumpkin stall. We needed some tiny pumpkins to decorate the inside of the house.

"Can we get a big pumpkin too?" Polly asked.

"Let's wait and buy one at the supermarket. It'll be too heavy to carry right now."

We were in the middle of the market when I glanced down to the end. Someone in a faded red sweatshirt with bushy hair was hurrying away. Him, again. Who was he? And why did he keep showing up? I wondered if he was linked to the poisoning, as the police had suggested when they announced their search. I couldn't drag Polly along after him to find out, and I didn't want to stare and have to explain why I was interested. He'd appeared out of nowhere like the ghosts in last night's movie. I remembered that the color red had run throughout the movie as a sign of threat. A red tent, a red sweater, a red balloon had kept me on edge. The sight of the reddish shirt today had given me a start. I laid my hand on Polly's arm just to steady myself.

"Let's look at some sunflowers for the house, okay?"

★ ★ ★

I sat at my study desk, blank pages of paper before me and my turquoise container of sharpened pencils to one side. Having dropped Polly off for her afternoon at school and having arranged the saucer-sized sunflowers in a vase, I was ready to work. The movie I'd seen with Wilmer the evening before, and now the disturbing reappearance of the figure in red, were haunting me, much like the poisoned corn bread. And that had given me an idea. I would write about haunting—how cuisines, like places, might be haunted by cultures of the past that were otherwise barely visible.

I'd eaten shrimp and grits three months earlier at a conference in Atlanta, and the spiciness of the dish had come as a surprise. As a Californian, I'd expected shrimp and grits to taste bland and had assumed this spicy, garlicky, andouille sausage and tomato-laden version was some new fusion cooking. Atlanta itself had struck me as less "Southern" than trendy and cosmopolitan, and the grits had seemed a part of that Atlanta vibe. But when a small group from the conference had decided to go on a three-day side visit to Savannah, the city had struck me as very "Southern" indeed. "Southern," I realized, meant "Old South" to me.

I'd been amazed to see the many ghost tours being advertised in Savannah, and I'd asked our guide why there seemed to be an obsession with ghosts in the city's culture.

"Because Savannah's haunted," the guide said with a straight face. She was a young woman with a water bottle, a visor, and a wry sense of humor. I'd lifted my eyebrows.

"Because we like to drink a lot and tell stories."

Later, having seen shrimp and grits on several menus, I asked how grits had entered Southern cuisine.

"Honestly, I don't know. You just eat the danged things."

Savannah did feel haunted, not by ghosts precisely, but by the presence in my imagination of what I didn't see. I'd read John Berendt's *Midnight in the Garden of Good and Evil* and felt phantom traces of its eccentric characters—one rambled through town with flies circling around his head (they were attached by threads). Most of all, however, Savannah had seemed haunted by slavery, a history that was strangely invisible in a city which had been a major port for the slave trade.

The next day, our group visited the only slave quarters open to the public. The ceiling of a downstairs room retained some of its original blue paint. "Haint blue," the docent told us, a color meant to ward off spirits. It struck me, then, that one root of Savannah's compulsive interest in ghosts must have been the culture of its West African slaves. In the gift shop I'd found a copy of a book on slave cooking, which mentioned that slave rations included corn and that some dishes made from Indian corn were similar to those that had been made in West Africa. Grits were often made from Indian corn.

The slave recipe for "Sawsidge" was similar to the recipe for the andouille version. And, later, I would learn that the cuisine of Gullah Geechee freed slaves, who lived on the islands near Savannah, included a good deal of Georgia shrimp. That spicy shrimp and grits I'd fallen for, far from being a recently minted cuisine, had deep roots in slave cultures of the past. What had seemed "new" to me in Atlanta was in fact old. What had seemed hidden in Savannah appeared on its menus. It was similar to the way ancient Native peoples lived on at Arbor State—in the name of its creek, in many of the arboretum's plants, in the soil that had once served as burial ground, and in the worldviews of Native American colleagues, some of whom, like Frank Walker, still cited their ancestors from a thousand years ago. The lives of an oppressed people could deeply shape a dominant culture. Even when those far-off lives were covered over, their presence continued like a kind of haunting. Turning that into a coherent essay was a challenge. But the idea of food and haunting haunted me.

It was late afternoon by the time I got up from my desk. I was tired of shrimp and grits and longed to go for a walk. I let myself into the garden, where a Delta Breeze had given the day an autumnal feel. Fall was a time of year I loved. As a child, it had meant going back to school and getting away from a lonely situation at home. As a teenager, it had meant release from a series of dreary summer jobs—selling clothes in a local shop or working for Sears Service Company. School had been my life and love, and its association with fall remained strong.

I thought of my date with Wilmer and of his physical reserve. Maybe I would call him and suggest a walk together. It would be a less formal way of being together and maybe he'd feel more at ease.

"Wilmer," I said on the phone, "it's Emily Addams. It's a beautiful day right now. Would you be interested in a walk on the greenbelt?"

"I'll be right over."

★ ★ ★

The greenbelt path wound its way through gently rolling lawns, then along some open fields, occasionally planted with tomatoes, past a large pond, surrounded by trees, and then through grassy mounds again. Wilmer looked especially appealing in a black T-shirt and light-colored pants. It pleased me that he had a sense of style, that he hadn't worn the usual khaki shorts and vapid polo shirts that were so common. As we walked along the fields, I saw a black bird with a flash of red and yellow swoop down to rest on a telephone wire.

"A red-winged black bird," Wilmer said.

"Are you a bird-watcher?"

"Yes, my ex-wife and I did a lot of bird-watching. And so did the man she ran off with."

"What went wrong?" I couldn't help asking. I was finding Wilmer attractive.

"I guess I was away too much. Math is competitive. You have to get your work out there, go to conferences, present at universities. I thought she was happy to be home with the kids."

What would I have felt in the wife's situation? Maybe I'm different, I thought. I have my own career. But a doubt lingered.

"So, she was lonely?"

"I guess. I went to Buenos Aires for six months to study with an expert in chaos theory. I wanted her to come too, but she didn't want to take the kids out of school. When I came back, she'd met someone else."

Wilmer's eyes looked moist. So there was pain for him. Maybe that explained his caution. We'd reached the pond where a large black lab, muddied and swampy from its swim, was shaking water all over a girl holding its leash. Sadie had often done the same to me.

"I know something of what you feel," I said. "I was furious with my ex-husband for most of our marriage, but when we separated, losing the family was such a blow that I kept thinking I should be admitted to a hospital." It seemed I was crossing some divide with Wilmer. He was a man who felt deeply but kept it under wraps. I felt myself liking him, feeling a connection. I bonded with those who'd lost someone dear to them. I'd lost Miriam, after all, and my family with Solomon and Polly, and before that I'd been the child of distant and hardly ever present parents.

"How competitive is mathematics?" I said, steering us back to lighter grounds.

I wasn't sure just yet how much personal revelation Wilmer, who was looking pained, would find comfortable.

"Very, and it extends outside the math."

"How so?"

"Some of my colleagues are really into biking, and they like to outdo each other. I used to keep up with them. I used to ride for three hours and then carry my bicycle up five flights of stairs." Wilmer laughed ruefully. "But my knees are getting bad, and, now, younger faculty whizz right past me. I've stopped riding the bike to school."

"That's a shame," I said. "I mean about the competitive culture of mathematics." Wilmer looked wistful. It wasn't the first time I was glad to be part of a more communal campus group like my own. "I love the greenbelt." I tried again to brighten our conversation. "What a wonderful idea to connect neighborhoods with hills and paths and fields. And Sadie loves the pond. She won't go into the swimming pool, but she swims in the pond. It's hard to get her out."

"She can probably feel the bottom of the pond as she goes in. Knowing she has some solid ground to return to lets her take chances."

"You're right." I often felt that way myself. My childhood had left me without a solid grounding in familial love, and I sometimes wondered how I would have felt in times of stress had I had that emotional foundation—as I assumed other people did. I was curious about Wilmer.

"What was your family like?" I asked.

"My father left us when I was a small child, though not before trying to kidnap me. I grew up with my mother." Wilmer looked into the distance.

So there had been family trauma for Wilmer too. No wonder I felt drawn to him.

"How about yours?" he asked.

"I was isolated as a child. My mother never bonded with me, and since my parents taught dancing seven nights a week, I barely saw them. I was never rooted in a sense of family." I glanced at Wilmer who was looking concerned. "I think that's why communities and other kinds of connections are so important to me." Wilmer looked at me kindly as if we had suddenly become friends. Then, we were silent for a moment.

"Some real thought went into planning this greenbelt," I said at last. "It's one of the things I really like about Arborville, the mindfulness that went into creating some of its communities." We had reached another soft patch of rolling lawn. "In the early evenings, whole families come out to walk. Once I saw a man and a woman followed by two children. The two children were being followed by two dogs, and at the end of the line I saw what appeared to be the family cat." Wilmer and I both laughed. I was glad to see he had a sense of humor. "I've never seen a cat trailing behind a family like that. It was sweet, but unusual for a feline."

I told Wilmer about my encounter with the man in red at the farmer's market.

"Are you sure he's homeless? There are a lot of odd characters on our campus."

"That's true." I liked the way Wilmer opened up new perspectives. There *was* something familiar about the man in red, but try as I might, I couldn't think what.

We finished our greenbelt walk where we'd begun, at my front door.

"That was a good walk," he said.

"Yes. Something to drink?" I asked as I opened the door.

"Water would be good."

I poured two glasses for us. Wilmer stood close to me as we drank and chatted for a few minutes.

"I should let you get back to work," Wilmer said. There it was again. Was he going to leave me again without so much as a handshake?

Wilmer stood before me, sweaty but broad shouldered and still stylish in his black shirt, and on an impulse, half-mischievous, half-friendly, I put my arms around his shoulders to give him a modest hug. Suddenly, Wilmer was kissing me. We stood there kissing for a long time and then moved to the couch. His body was slender and wiry. He obviously spent time in the gym, and he smelled pleasantly of Old Spice. We sat there together for a long time. After the pain of my divorce, it was delicious to be in a man's arms again. Later, we got ourselves more water.

"This is a surprise. The first time we went out you didn't even touch me. What happened?"

He blushed.

"I've only been dating for a few months and I've met some cautious women. One woman I dated let me have it when I touched her. She had some issue about being touched. I know you're a feminist. I didn't want to insult you too."

"There are many kinds of feminists. I like to be touched."

Wilmer smiled broadly with something more than relief.

"That's good to know."

★ ★ ★

I dressed in my gym clothes, picked up my gym bag, and got in the car. Although I'd taken a long walk with Wilmer that afternoon, it was the night of my kickboxing class at a gym on the eastern edge of town, and I never missed it. The instructor, a young woman with a shiny, black ponytail, was small but well-muscled and wore a two-piece, hot pink leotard which showed off her amazing abs. She often discussed her social life with the class, commented on the color of her students' toenail polish, and worked us so vigorously that we had to mop up the floor from our sweat. Her workouts were the hardest I'd ever experienced. It surprised me what my body was willing to do under my instructor's cheerful, hard-driving spell.

Since I was only an average kickboxer, I stood in the middle of the large square room, in which a mirror covered the entire front wall. The more advanced students—those who could do a roundhouse kick while tucking one foot beneath them and leaping into the air—stood to the left. To do a plain right roundhouse you had to lean over the left foot. Then you lifted your right leg at an exact right angle from your body, turned your pointed right foot so that the top of it—but not the toes—would contact the bag, and then extended the right leg forcefully, smacking the bag with all your strength. The round-house maneuver was difficult enough without the jumping.

A woman in her twenties stood to my left, slender with long reddish hair and a skilled boxer. She worked at Arbor State, and I sometimes wondered what fueled the fierceness of that long red ponytail whopping back and forth. She'd mastered the roundhouse with the leap and came at the bag like a char-acter in a martial arts movie, her left leg folded, her right leg flying into the bag. My own left foot stayed firmly glued to the ground even when I tried to think it upward. I consoled myself by thinking it was probably a wise foot, that it knew more than I did.

Half the class consisted of grueling repetitions: left front kick, pivot, right roundhouse. Then right front kick, pivot, left roundhouse, repeat, repeat, repeat. Next, pummeling the bag, right cross, left cross, and jab over and over. Then squatting against the wall to work the stomach and the thighs. Finally, down to the floor for push-ups. Twenty, then twenty more.

"You can do it," the instructor called out. She was pushing her own body up and down, up and down with ease. These sessions left me exhausted although they were an excellent way to work off my frustrations with the university.

After class, I walked into the parking lot, the cold air shock-ing my sweaty body like a Nordic plunge. I'd parked my car on the far end of the darkened lot, and as I walked toward it, I noticed a dark blue van, the very kind of car that had followed Tess. My stomach contracted. There are lots of blue vans, I told myself evenly. But I hurried toward my car just the same. Looking into the rearview mirror, I started the engine. The red-haired boxer appeared briefly in the light of the doorway and then moved in my direction. I relaxed and began to back out. As I turned toward the exit, the fierce boxer reached the blue van and disappeared. Was she the owner of the van? Could an employee of the university be a member of Save the Fields? Was that what lay behind her intensity with the bag? There are lots of blue vans, I told myself once more.

Driving home in darkness, I wondered whether kickboxing could really be a form of self-defense. My uneasiness about the poisoning and now the man in red had prompted me to engage in fantasies of how I might use it, how I would strike an attacker with a left front kick to the stomach and then follow the front kick with a totally surprising roundhouse from the right. Would my body remember the moves I'd so often practiced? I hoped I'd never have occasion to find out. What I did know was that after a long walk with Wilmer and a kickboxing class as well I'd sleep soundly that night.

But at 3:00 a.m. the sharp *brring* of the phone broke through my slumber.

"Hullo," I said groggily. There was only silence on the other end.

Wild Georgia Shrimp and Grits

5–6 tablespoons unsalted butter, divided

2 cups thinly sliced Vidalia onion (about 2 medium onions)

1¾ cups half and half

3½ cups chicken broth, divided

1½ cups stone-ground grits (Riverview Farms recommended)

½ teaspoon granulated garlic

½ teaspoon granulated sugar

1 tablespoon finely chopped garlic

1 cup chopped andouille sausage (about ¼ pound)

1 14-ounce can chopped San Marzano tomatoes

½ pound fresh Georgia shrimp, peeled and deveined

¼ cup finely chopped assorted herbs (oregano, thyme, marjoram, and parsley)

Kosher salt and finely ground pepper

In a large sauté pan, heat 2 tablespoons butter over medium heat and swirl to coat the bottom of the pan. Add onions and heat until they start to soften, about 5 minutes.

Reduce heat and let the onions cook 20 minutes without stirring. If the onions start to brown, give them a quick stir and reduce the heat. After 20 minutes, stir the onions and continue to cook, stirring only occasionally, until the onions have caramelized.

In a large saucepan, bring the half and half and 2 cups chicken broth to a boil. Slowly, whisk in the grits and return to a boil. Reduce heat to a simmer and cook the grits about 30 minutes over low heat, stirring often. If the grits become too thick, add a little half and half or broth. When the grits are done, they will be soft and creamy but a little al dente.

Season the grits with granulated garlic, a pinch of sugar, and salt and pepper to taste. Add 1–2 tablespoons butter.

When the grits are cooking, add the garlic to the caramelized onions and increase the heat to medium-high. Cook until garlic is fragrant, about 1 minute.

Scrape onion mixture to the side of the pan and add the sausage. Let the sausage cook for 5–7 minutes, turning to brown on both sides.

Add tomatoes and remaining chicken broth and bring to a boil. Reduce the heat to a simmer. Allow mixture to reduce and thicken, about 10 minutes.

Add shrimp; cook until just curled and opaque, about 4 minutes. Stir in the remaining 2 tablespoons of butter, herbs, and salt and pepper to taste.

Adapted by permission of Ron Eyester.

Chapter 8

I stuck my hand in my purse to find my keys, stabbed my finger on a lurking pencil, and raked through an unpleasant combination of loose change and crumbs until I grasped the thick ring and finally entered my office. I really did need to stop storing half-eaten scones in my purse, no matter how well wrapped. But other thoughts were pulling at the edge of my consciousness. Who had called me in the middle of the night? A wrong number? Someone harassing me? And why? I'd been alone in the house the evening before. A house full of glass. Sliding doors in the main room opened to the yard, as did French doors in my bedroom and in my study on the other side of the home. I loved the light they provided during the day, but at night, alone, they sometimes made me feel edgy. It was easy to break through glass.

Seeking something else to absorb my attention, I sat at my desk and turned on the computer. It was probably a wrong number, I told myself. Let's see if the calls continue. There was an e-mail from Tess: "My turn to be questioned." My throat constricted as I tried to think about the logic the police might be pursuing. Tess hadn't been at the reception, so the police must be following another thread. Tess, of course, *had* been on the panel, but, once again, I wondered if the police were aware of that. And, if they were, what kind of murderous motivation could they have attributed to someone as wholesome as homemade bread? Though lately, I had to admit, even innocent things, like pigs and corn bread, had taken on sinister associations. Still, while Tess was forthright and passionate about her views, she was also rational. She'd argued with Peter, and her manner had been forceful, but she hadn't been confrontational like Juan Carlos. Maybe, the police were questioning people who were interested in GMOs or maybe they, like me, were fishing for leads.

There was also an e-mail from Grace Chen, another colleague in Women's Studies and a professor in Asian American Studies as well: "I have something I'd like to talk to you about. Could we meet as soon as possible? It would be best to meet face-to-face."

"I'll be right up," I typed. I walked up the back stairs to the third floor where Asian American had a long row of offices.

★ ★ ★

"How are you, my dear?" Grace said, as she ushered me in. "Let's sit on the couch." Grace, with her oval face and glossy black bob, had somehow made room for a blue plush sofa and a coffee table across from her desk. A vase of peach-colored lilies stood on the table, and there was a blue figured carpet on the floor. It was like the living room of your favorite aunt, I thought, or of your therapist. I'd been to several therapists over the years. It also reminded me of Miriam's living rooms, which were always offbeat but elegant and comforting. A white couch, large blue printed pillows, flowers—often white peonies.

Grace was another hard worker. She tended to the needs of the program's students and to the faculty's as well, and, despite her junior status, was frequently pressed to act as chair. Directing a program, of course, took time away from writing and publishing, which were the real priorities in advancing one's career, but running a program was a job Grace enjoyed and at which she excelled. She had a subtle touch in negotiations and even when angry she could look composed. She'd taught me to be more patient, to stay more calm when difficult situations arose.

"It's good to see you." I gave her a hug, and the two of us settled into the soft blue cushions.

"A student came to me, yesterday, a senior, a minor in Asian American, who is doing pre-vet. Her name's Mei Lee. Have you had her in class?"

"No, I haven't met her."

"Mei Lee's family is very traditional. They came from China when she was twelve." Grace paused as if gathering herself together. "She told me something that you must keep in the strictest confidence. Her parents would pull her out of the university if they ever knew." I nodded.

"Mei Lee is an intern at the Hog Barn, and it's one of her duties to feed the pigs in the morning, including Peter Elliott's. His pigs are young, and Mei Lee felt an interest in them because, you know, young pigs are cute." Grace looked for a moment into the peach-colored centers of the lilies. "Here's where it gets difficult. Peter was always in and out checking on the pigs, and he and Mei Lee grew close. I think she felt isolated at the barn, and, well, one thing led to another, and she began having an affair with Peter."

"In the Hog Barn?" How would that work? I wondered. What is there to lie on? Bales of hay? No, that's a different sort of barn.

"In Peter's office, I think, which is not far away. But a few months ago, he began to act preoccupied. He'd lost interest in her, or that's what Mei Lee thought, and their relationship had become strained. Mei Lee looks delicate—her parents call her "beautiful plum"—but she can be quite angry. They argued and she cut things off. When she came down to feed the hogs that morning and saw Peter lying near one of the pig's pens, it came as a terrible shock."

"Like losing him twice."

"You can't tell anyone about this," Grace said, looking through her narrow glasses. "If her family had any idea, they'd be outraged, and everything she's worked for would be lost. She's a senior, and it's vital she finish out the year, but she's in a terrible state. I knew you were aware she'd been at the Hog Barn the morning they found Peter, so I wanted to talk with you before you'd told more people." Grace leaned toward me, putting a gentle hand on my arm. "I hope we can protect her by keeping this quiet."

"How'd you know that I knew about her?"

"Helena told me." News circulated fast on the women's network.

"I'll keep quiet about Mei Lee. No need to punish her even more. Besides Peter's in a coma. But this will cost him a good deal when it comes out. Sleeping with an undergraduate!"

The strong fragrance of the lilies began to tickle my nose.

"Right now, it would cost Mei Lee more."

"She's lucky to have you." From my soft bower in the couch I could see a picture on Grace's desk of a short, white-haired woman and a dark-haired one wearing long flowery dresses and standing in front of a mango tree, the orange-red fruit hanging from long stems like festive lanterns. I knew they were Grace's grandmother and mother, who lived on the Big Island of Hawaii. It was a heritage that Grace loved and honored. As in her native state, she wore sandals all year round despite the fact that winters in Arborville were both wet and cold.

"Do you know," I inquired, "if the student quarters in the Hog Barn have an oven? I ask because if Mei Lee's real relationship to Peter were to become known to the police, it would make her a suspect in his poisoning."

Grace wrinkled her nose. "I doubt they have an oven, don't you? But at any rate Mei Lee isn't into baking or cooking. She lives on takeout. And I'm virtually certain she had nothing to do with Peter's poisoning. The police questioned her that morning but, of course, she only told them about feeding Peter's pigs."

"I'd like to find out whether she has access to an oven in the barn. If she doesn't, it might help at some point to put her in the clear."

"How will you find that out?"

"I'll schedule a tour of the Hog Barn. I'll say I'm writing a book on food production. How's that?"

"Clever." Grace looked at me with admiration. "You do have a knack for gathering information."

"I'll let you know what I find." Grace was so warmhearted toward her students that she would find it nearly impossible to suspect Mei Lee, but I, having never met the young woman, wasn't so sure. I wanted to know more. Mei Lee, of course, could have bought corn bread and poisoned it. That would be difficult to trace, but the question of the oven could be easily resolved.

★ ★ ★

As I approached the Hog Barn, it struck me with greater force than before that its yards lay open to the sky just ninety feet outside the Institute for Analytical Dynamics, where Wilmer worked. I felt a connection with Wilmer now, a man who'd been afraid to even touch me, but that the Hog Barn and the Institute lay virtually side by side gave me a moment's pause— until the memory of Old Spice and wiry arms diverted me and I brushed the thought aside. I, myself, after all, had been in Bauman Hall the night before Peter was found, and Bauman was almost as close to the Hog Barn as Analytical Dynamics. Proximity to the scene of a crime wasn't proof of anything.

Like most on campus, I hadn't the foggiest idea of what "Analytical Dynamics" meant, but I knew that it was housed in an impressive building, boasting an entire wall of reflective glass, and I knew that important visitors in math and science were frequently brought within its precincts. The Institute, now absorbing the blinding sun in its black and mirrorlike wall, seemed a symbol of the future—just as Wilmer had observed— and the Hog Barn, with its dull red siding, dirt-brown shingles, and marshy pens, seemed a vestige of the past, an emblem of a more modest time when Arbor State had been no more than a university farm with a long horizon. The proximity of the Institute to the Hog Barn had become a campus joke and, to some, a professional embarrassment. I wondered if Wilmer, despite his country origins, had found it painful at times to parade distinguished visitors past these reeking sties and lolling, fleshy forms.

Although the odor from the yards had pierced my nostrils, I moved in closer to study the enormous pigs, which, lying on their sides and exposing their bellies to the air, appeared to have surrendered themselves to the oppressive heat. I'd always found these hogs a pleasing eccentricity. Their mud-encrusted bodies sprawled in the middle of what had slowly become a futuristic landscape of expensive buildings—all devoted to science and technology. It had made me laugh to see the hogs lay claim to expensive real estate, like country cousins lounging on the doorstep of a tony family with suitcases tied in string.

That a high-ranked professor had been found face down and poisoned among these icons of rural innocence was like a bad dream—or, more to the point, a bad joke. But the joke was now on me. Who would have thought ten days ago that I would have become embroiled with the Hog Barn and its inhabitants or that I myself would be under suspicion of poisoning someone I barely knew? If Peter were to regain consciousness, of course, the whole case would be laid out at once. He would know where he had gotten corn bread and that would be that. I could redirect my energies to other matters, such as Polly and my work and hopefully Wilmer Crane, and I could stop fretting about unexpected visits from police.

I walked to the wide double doors of the entrance where a young woman was already waiting. She was not Mei Lee, but a stout blonde.

"Thanks so much for giving me this tour," I said.

"No problem. We do this all the time. My name's Heather. The first room we'll see is for the farrowing sows." We entered the reception room and turned left through long strips of plastic that acted as a kind of curtain. The smell of pig and pig waste hit my nose like a foul wind. I had trouble breathing.

"It takes some getting used to," Heather said. "We keep these sows for farrowing."

I looked into the concrete pens with interest. Giant pink pigs with black patches lay on their sides in some twenty pens, with fifteen to twenty piglets attached to their teats. Some of the baby pigs were squealing loudly as they struggled to find a nipple. I wondered how Heather and Mei Lee could bear to hear those shrieks, the cries of creatures desperate to eat, desperate to survive. I found it unnerving, though being a mother and considerably older than the young woman in front of me, I probably thought more about mortality than she.

Heather picked up a piglet, which wailed piercingly. She held it closer to get it calm. I stroked its pale pink body, which was covered in fine white hairs. Its small round eyes looked out from pink circles of skin, giving it an air of surprise, and its ears were huge and a deeper pink than that of its body. Sweet, I thought. Baby animals always have such large ears. The piglet continued crying, and Heather was forced to put it back down in its pen.

"You see their tails," Heather said. "They're born with curly tails, but there's no feeling in the curl and they often bite each other's tails, and if there's blood, the other piglets will pick on the bloodied pig to establish hierarchy. So we cut off the curl before that happens. Pigs fight a lot until they've established dominance."

"Pigs fight?" This was the first I'd heard of it.

"Yes, they fight for the first teat. Usually the biggest male pig gets it. And then when they're older and are put in pens separate from their mothers, they fight again. That's why we put pigs from the same litter in a pen together. They fight far less that way."

"Do the sows fight too?"

"Yes, until they've settled on a hierarchy. But boars are especially aggressive. That's why we keep them in separate corrals." Heather looked down at her pig wards fondly. "Pigs are smart, though. They dung in a corner of the pen that is away from their food. And the reason they roll in the mud is to keep cool. They don't perspire, but the mud brings their body temperature down. People don't give pigs nearly enough credit."

I began to think so too. Heather led me to the outside pens where the pungent pig smell lightened.

"These are slightly older pigs," Heather said. "These are being fed an experimental genetically engineered food."

"How often are they fed?"

"These pigs have access to food whenever they want it."

I looked at the young pigs more closely. They'd been shy at first, backing away together, warily, in a mass, but now a few pushed forward sniffing in a friendly way through the metal bars. Their ears were still quite oversized, giving them the look of porcine kindergarteners. One looked up inquiringly, as if it might have questions of its own for me.

"Could you tell me about your duties?" I asked Heather.

Heather went on about the feeding, the hosing of the pens, the cleaning of the pig waste.

"And you live upstairs?" I wondered how it smelled up there.

"Yes, another girl and I do."

"How do you get on? Do you make meals? Do you have a kitchen? An oven?"

Heather snorted a laugh.

"We have a hot plate."

"Ah, so you don't bake." I was disappointed.

"No, we usually eat at the cafeteria or bring something in."

"Sounds like a challenging life."

"We don't get a lot of visitors upstairs."

I looked at the young pigs once again. More of them now were poking their noses through the bars, as if eager to get acquainted.

"But down here, do people go in and out for their work?"

"Yes, the Hog Barn is a busy place. Graduate students and faculty are in and out for their projects all the time."

Who knew? I thought. Someone other than Wilmer and Mei Lee might have visited the barn that morning along with Peter.

★ ★ ★

My clothes smelled of pig, but I returned to my office anyway and, on a whim, decided to stay late and finish the justification document for Women's Studies—this despite the fact that I was getting hungry. I'd purchased a corn muffin earlier that day and had forgotten to eat it. It had looked plump and delicious early in the morning, and, though it must be misshapen from a day spent among the books and papers in my rolling bag, it would tide me over. I rooted around in the bag to find it and then removed it from its paper sack. One of its sides had caved in, giving me pause. Should I be eating muffins I hadn't baked myself? Already salivating, I looked at it then tossed it in the trash. I was getting paranoid.

I could write documents touting Women's Studies in my sleep, but this latest round was particularly important. I needed to argue not just for my own program but for its interdependence with ethnic studies. I reviewed the questions I had to answer. What were the program's goals, how did they fit with the long-term priorities of the campus, what resources did the program need, what could be cut, how would I justify the continued funding of the program?

The university's stated priorities were so lofty and so broad that I had no trouble plugging the program in. The university claimed to be invested in diversity and transnational study. I could be utterly truthful when I wrote that one of the central goals of the program was to help make women's studies a field in which the important issues and questions were arrived at through dialogue across gender, racial, ethnic, sexual, class, and national divides. The women's studies program, I continued, had also worked with all the ethnic studies programs on campus to build close and fruitful ties, a strength we meant to build on in the future. The stark contradiction between the university's stated investment in "diversity" and its actions toward the women's and ethnic studies programs was a continuing source of somewhat bitter amusement to me and my colleagues.

Once I'd finished the document, I grew unsettled about the fact that it was dark and that I was still in Haven Hall. In the past few months several thefts had been reported. The programs had composed a letter of complaint to the administration, pointing out the thefts, repeating the staff's concerns with regard to their own safety, and urging the administration to move the lab to another building. The letter had produced a meeting with lower administration, but nothing whatsoever had been done. By day, Haven buzzed with life. Doors stood open, faculty clustered in the halls, and program offices swarmed with students. But by night the doors were shut, the lights were low, and you could hear your own footsteps in the empty corridors. The unsettling effects of *The Sixth Sense* had not worn off, and when I walked down the hall to the women's bathroom, I half expected to encounter a sudden, ghastly figure or the warning sign of red. I could feel my throat tightening, my heart beating in my chest. Staying past dark in Haven Hall had been a mistake. I would head home now.

I gathered my papers into their file folders, stuck the files into my rolling bag, and headed down to the main door. Outside, the moon was the size of a sliver and the quad was barely lit. For a moment, I thought of calling the campus escort service, which would have provided a student to walk me to my car, but the distant sight of two figures descending the library steps was reassuring. I was not alone. I walked toward the library and then turned left on Library Lane, staying on the right side of the street so as to be near the building.

I reached the edge of campus at Lupine Avenue and looked to my right. About a block away a wooded path lay in shadows between some squat, utilitarian-looking buildings, and a wild-haired man was walking toward me from it. There was no one else in sight, and I stood there for a moment, stunned. Then I felt for the keys at the bottom of my purse—stabbing myself on the same pencil and fingering the same crumbs as I had that morning—while the figure gained ground. I froze, then stopped groping for the keys, located my car in the near empty lot, glanced at the approaching figure, and finally began to run. Sprinting, I reached the driver's side, dumped the contents of my purse on the ground, felt for the keys, scraped everything back in, unlocked the door, threw myself in, relocked the doors, and started the engine. Through the front window I could see the man pause to look at me and then continue his solitary stroll. As he passed under one of the streetlights, I saw a glimpse of dusty red.

Backing out, I turned the car and aimed it straight across the parking lines toward the far exit, then turned right, passing a blue van. Instantly, the engine of the van started up and its lights turned on. I felt a spill of fear pass through my stomach. I glanced in my mirror, saw the van right behind me, and drove quickly down Mariposa Avenue, turning left on Poppy Lane and then left on Paintbrush Boulevard. The university's athletic fields lay in the darkness on one side and old houses, now devoted to fraternities and sororities, on the other. The van closed in. Don't panic! I told myself. This is a common way to get to the west and north of town. Nonetheless, I drove faster, and at the corner of Paintbrush Boulevard and Ceanothus Avenue I barreled through the yellow light to turn right. The blue van stopped.

I sped past the elementary school and the streets named for wild animals—Wild Deer Lane, Coyote Court, Badger Crossing—until I reached the maze of smaller streets with Spanish names. I reached my house, looked behind me, and hurried to the porch. It was hard to see the keyhole, and my hand was trembling. At last I put both hands on the key, guided it into the lock, and opened the door, stepping quickly inward. I locked the dead bolt, turned on the living room lights, and took refuge in the kitchen. I'd spooked myself and needed a glass of wine—maybe two.

That night I dreamed I was walking toward the water tower in the darkness. The moon was half full, and the tower's white cylinder and its ghostly legs glimmered pale as bones in the moon's muted light. Someone frightening, dressed in red, was chasing me. I began to climb the small white metal ladder to get away. But as I progressed, one hand over the other, one foot after the next, it occurred to me I'd made a horrible mistake. What had made me think the tower was a safe place to be? What if the red figure climbed after me? What if we reached the catwalk? There'd be nowhere else to go. I was deathly afraid of heights. How had I forgotten? Below me on the road, I saw a blue van in the darkness. It stopped and parked to the side of the water tower's northern legs. The van turned off its lights.

The shrill ring of the phone pierced my uneasy slumber. "Hello?" I said tentatively. Silence on the other end. I lay there, feeling a tingling in my arms and hands, until I fell into a shallow slumber.

Corn Muffins

Makes 12 muffins

2 cups of all-purpose flour
1 cup yellow cornmeal
  (stone-ground, whole
  grain)
1½ teaspoons baking
  powder
1 teaspoon baking soda
½ teaspoon salt

2 large eggs
¾ cup sugar
8 tablespoons (1 stick) of
  unsalted butter, melted
  and cooled
¾ cup sour cream
½ cup milk

Adjust an oven rack to the middle position and preheat oven to 400°F.

Generously coat a 12-cup muffin tin with Pam or other non-stick spray.

Whisk the flour, cornmeal, baking powder, baking soda, and salt together in a large bowl.

Whisk the eggs and sugar together in a medium bowl until combined. Whisk in the melted and cooled butter in three additions. Whisk in one half of the sour cream and milk until smooth, then whisk in the second half.

Gently fold the egg mixture into the flour mixture with a rubber spatula until just combined. Do not overmix.

Use a large ice-cream scoop or measuring cup, sprayed with Pam or other nonstick spray, to divide the batter evenly among the muffin cups. Do not level or flatten the surface of the mounds.

Bake until light golden brown and a toothpick inserted into the center of a muffin comes out with just a few crumbs attached (about 16–18 minutes).

Let the muffins cool in the pan for 5 minutes, then flip out onto a wire rack and let cool for 10 minutes before serving.

Adapted by permission of Mel at Mel's Kitchen Cafe
http://www.melskitchencafe.com/cornbread-muffins/.

Chapter 9

Isobel's face looked like a cloud full of rain. Had something happened? I'd come to her office the next morning to seek advice about the figure in red, the blue van, and the ringing phone. Were they connected or were they a series of frightening coincidences? The call had been the most disturbing. Someone knew my number, knew how to invade the safe enclosure of my home in the middle of the night. But why? Did the calls have to do with Peter's poisoning, with my unsuccessful attempts to identify the poisoner, or were they more random, perhaps another version of the threats and harassments that single women often encountered?

Isobel was strong, also wise. She might have insights that would put me at rest, or, now that a roasting spit seemed to have lodged itself in my back, my throat, and head, she might guide me, in thinking about what to do. Isobel hugged me and the two of us sat down.

"You seem upset," I said.

"It's the time of year. It takes me back to something painful."

I looked at her expectantly.

"I've never told you about my nephew, my sister's son. It was two years ago, the year I was so angry."

"I remember. I couldn't get you to talk to me."

"Something had happened. Years ago my sister married a

man living on the reservation." I'd never seen this reservation, although it was only thirty miles away.

"Her husband took to drinking, and so she worked and raised her son herself. I offered to help with child care, and, over the years, my nephew and I became very close." Isobel began to rock her body back and forth ever so slightly, as if the motion stilled something inside of her. "It was his last year of high school. He'd had a tough time in local schools. He looked Mexican, but he didn't speak Spanish, and so he was an outsider to Mexicans and whites both." Isobel's rocking became more pronounced. "He wanted to drop out. I guess he thought he'd tend to grapes for a living. He was already working harvests. I told him, 'You can't just throw your life away.' I began to spend more time mentoring him."

"You would do that. You mentor most of the students in your program." Isobel gave me a thankful look.

"He began to do better. He was going to graduate in the spring, but that November, after I'd taken him to a celebration of El Dia de Los Muertos, he was found in his car early in the morning, his body full of drugs." Tears filled Isobel's eyes. "It was before the casino had taken off. There was a lot of poverty on the Res, a lot of drinking, a lot of drugs, and no resources for young people or anyone really."

I felt my own eyes fill.

"I didn't know he was into drugs. I kept thinking that I should have known, should have saved him."

"He was like your child. I can't imagine any greater sorrow than losing a child." I felt a stab of pain. What if I were ever to lose Polly?

"I was so angry that year. We've lost so much—our land, much of our culture, our lives. Indian populations were deci-mated after white men arrived in California. And then to have him taken from me like that and from the rest of his family. He'd been cut down, poisoned by our history and by the life imposed on him. And I was angry at myself that I hadn't prevented it."

"You did your best. That's all anyone can do." I thought of how I'd worried about being a better friend to Miriam. I put my hand on top of Isobel's and told her how sorry I was.

I understood now, in a more visceral way, why mentoring and protecting the vulnerable were so important to Isobel. I felt closer to her, she who'd always seemed so strong and self-controlled. You didn't have to be blood-related to feel connection.

"Why did you come by this morning?" Isobel wiped her cheeks with her free hand.

"I was frightened," I said and began to tell her about the events of the night before, but now my own worries, once so bold in my imagination, seemed to fade alongside Isobel's deep-dyed grief.

★ ★ ★

Six men, one woman—all white, all in the sciences—sat like headstones at a heavy, wooden table, reading binders. It was afternoon by now, and I'd arrived for my first meeting as a participant in the Super Committee, a group that nominated members to all the faculty committees on campus. I had some thoughts about what I would try to do as its newest associate. I'd prepared myself for the meeting by reading and analyzing the committee's membership rolls over the last twenty years, and thus I knew I was the only current member not in the sciences. That was bad enough, but I had been surprised to learn that the Super Committee had had no representatives from social science for half of the past twenty years and no representatives from the humanities for almost as long.

The Super Committee and, therefore, most of the committees on campus had been staffed by mainly white male scientists, with, yes, a few white women scientists thrown in, and it was easy to understand why. Men in science tended to know other men in science and felt confident sharing power with them. It was clearer now why it had been so hard to get new courses in Women's Studies approved. There'd been no one on the Education Committee who had had any familiarity with work outside the sciences. I'd been appalled by my findings. Things on the Super Committee were far worse than I'd imagined.

"We need to get started," the chair of the committee said. She was a woman scientist with straight black eyebrows like the wings of a raven. I opened my own binder. It contained lists of committees and the names of members past and present.

"Our first order of business is to nominate members to the Promotion Committee." Since this committee voted on the promotions and tenure of every faculty member on campus, only full professors with a lot of clout would do. I raised my hand—I'd prepared for this as well.

"I'd like to nominate Antonio Conti, director of Native American Studies. He's a high-ranking full professor and has an international reputation. He's been a consultant for several projects with the United Nations." A ripple of consternation passed over one of my colleague's face. Two others moved in their seats.

"I don't think he's the right man for the job," Collin Morehead said.

In his fifties, Collin reminded me of a picture I'd once seen of a bulldog's face superimposed on the body of a man wearing a checkered shirt. I remembered Collin from the panel the previous spring. Like Peter, he worked on GMOs. I wondered what kind of relationship they had had. "Think more about C.M.," I wrote in a tiny script on the top of my pad of paper.

"Conti once wrote an angry letter to the Promotion Committee about something he claimed was an injustice on their part. We can't nominate someone like that to the committee." Collin, an Australian, seemed to chew upon his words as if worrying a large bone.

"If he was angry about injustice," I ventured, "isn't that a good thing? Don't we want someone with a critical perspective on the work of the committee?"

"Well, yes," another of the scientists broke in, a gaunt man with white hair and round glasses, "but not someone who's angry about it."

God forbid we should be angry. I thought. God forbid we should have someone who really cares about injustice.

"It's important to diversify the committees, however," I persisted. "Professor Conti would bring both scholarly and philosophical diversity."

Raven eyebrows, chair of the committee, looked as if she'd been slapped.

"I hope you're not suggesting that we care nothing about diversity," she said.

"Of course not, but I've read through the membership rolls over the last twenty years, and it's been almost entirely white."

Collin pursed his lips as if he had just taken a bite of a bad ham sandwich.

"We've certainly put women on committees," he blustered. He grew larger in his chair, the buttons of his shirt straining to encase his stomach—as if it were a sausage swelling in a microwave.

"Yes," I said, "I've actually counted them."

Collin squinted his small eyes at me. The stark rejection of Antonio, whom I knew to be a good and highly qualified man, said a lot about the myopia of some with power in the university, but I decided not to press Antonio's case. There'd be plenty of other nominations, and I didn't want to alienate my fellow committee members so completely and so soon. I'd already violated an unwritten law for outsiders such as myself: don't call attention to the status quo. It wasn't just a question of changing it. They didn't want to know about it either. But there was still the budget committee and I had two names on my list—one a full professor in Asian American and the other a full professor in African American studies. I was white and could use race privilege to help make the university a more equitable place, but despite, or even because of that, I was growing a reputation for acting out of line.

★ ★ ★

I walked the arboretum path seeking to restore a sense of peace, but after my struggles on the Super Committee, even the ducks sipping at their puddle didn't comfort me much today. I'd reached the farthest bridge once again, when strolling toward me through the redwood path was the man with the reddish sweatshirt and wild pirate's beard whom I'd seen three times before. He was looking up at the tall trees. This time, my adrenalin spiked, I didn't stop but walked deliberately toward him. I came within six feet and stopped.

I always mistook him for a homeless man—Professor Ned Goldman of Entomology, who spent his life outdoors studying butterflies. He'd been on sabbatical for a year, and I'd all but forgotten him, but even when he hadn't been away, I always had trouble recognizing who he was at first. Constant exposure to the sun had turned his skin the color of a walnut and lined his face with wrinkles, and he always seemed to be dressed for working in the fields. But the look was not just practical. I was aware that Ned cultivated a certain eccentricity. The wild frizz of cinnamon-colored hair and beard were deliberate. He liked throwing people into confusion with his looks the way he liked writing essays that overthrew conventional assumptions, and he'd certainly succeeded in confusing me.

I remembered a paper I'd happened upon while searching the Internet for hints on how to create a butterfly-friendly garden. Some local butterflies, Ned had argued, fed on plants that were regarded as invasive species. If butterflies were good, as most people assumed, how could you regard the plants they fed on as something bad? You couldn't have the butterflies without the invasive plants. Conventional wisdom about the matter was not complex enough.

How many times had I seen him and gone through this shock of suddenly realizing who he was? He attended talks of every kind all over campus, even those in Women's Studies, and yet I never knew him from a distance.

"Hello, Emily."

"How are you, Ned? Welcome back. Are you stalking butterflies?"

"Nope, just taking my short cut to the arboretum. I live near campus and I like to walk through this redwood grove to reach the creek. Did you know these groves were planted in the 1930s? Some of the trees are two hundred and twenty-five feet high."

"No, I didn't know that. Do you find butterflies here?"

"Not really. But it's a good place. I like to be near these trees."

"I can understand that. Well good to see you, Ned."

"Have a good day."

The man in red was Ned Goldman! Talk about a person who looked like an invasive species. But would Ned tear up a cornfield or poison someone? I doubted that very much.

★ ★ ★

I sat in my office, chagrined at my failure to recognize Ned and at my assumption that someone who looked like an outsider was necessarily a danger. But I couldn't dwell upon that now. I still had my seminar in popular culture to teach. Today, I was beginning a section on how to analyze a magazine. My focus was on the way magazines respond to social anxieties by offering their readers desirable identities and a sense of community, both of which could make readers feel better about themselves and the way they led their lives. I, myself, loved popular magazines and was addicted to ones on homes and gardens and now food. Miriam had been a reader of *Architectural Digest,* but I preferred the more approachable *Sunset Magazine.* I read it eagerly as a way of participating in the sensuous and relaxed existence that I often didn't have time to live. I cut out plans for ambitious gardens that I lacked the time to lay out and clipped endless recipes that I never cooked. But clipping the recipes made me feel as if, perhaps, I had cooked them after all.

Of late, I had taken to teaching a magazine on Asian American popular culture. Many of my Women's Studies students were Asian American, and teaching the magazine was a way of engaging them in the course, of understanding the relations between race and gender, and of making Asian American culture visible to the class as a whole. One result of using this material was that I was always well informed about Asian American entertainers. I could tell you a lot about the early years of Michelle Yeoh, Jet Li, and Adam Saruwatari. There were no recipes, unfortunately, but there were occasional references to food like cornmeal pancakes with kumquats for which I had found directions on the Internet. The kumquats were candied in honey and coconut milk, then served on top of pancakes with a coconut syrup. It was a recipe I'd been dying to try.

I'd just settled into my office chair when there was a knock on the door. I rose to open it and stood face-to-face with Sergeants Gina Garcia and Dorothy Brown. I showed them in, and they sat at the small round table I kept in my office for meetings.

"We have further results," Dorothy said eagerly. "The lab found traces of onion and goat cheese too. Does anyone else you know make this recipe?"

"Not that I know of, but I got it online and modified it a bit, so plenty of people could have had access to something similar. There are dozens of recipes for corn bread I'm beginning to understand. I thought for a minute. "You know, choosing this particular recipe becomes meaningful in view of the fact that there *are* so many recipes for corn bread. If someone else bought the corn bread or made it, why didn't they buy or make plain corn bread or corn bread with chilies? Why use corn bread with trendy ingredients like goat cheese and caramelized onions? My impression is that you can't buy that kind of corn bread in Arborville, so either someone used a piece of mine as a vessel for the poison or went out of their way to make corn bread that was similar."

"I see what you mean," Gina said.

"Would anyone want to throw suspicion on you?" Dorothy asked.

"That never occurred to me," I said. Did I have enemies I didn't know about? I'd certainly irritated my colleagues on the Super Committee by pressing Antonio's nomination and then by successfully nominating both the professor of African and of Asian American Studies to the powerful Committee on Budgets, but that was too recent to explain much. Who else had I angered in the past? And would someone I'd annoyed go so far as to make anonymous phone calls at 3:00 a.m.?

"There's something else I wanted to tell you. I've been getting phone calls in the middle of the night. Is there anything the police can do about that?"

Dorothy and Gina glanced at each other.

"We've had some experience in that area," Dorothy said. "You can have the phone company transfer late night calls to a religious call line. That usually stops the caller cold."

"I'm going to try that." It had never occurred to me that the phone company could be so obliging.

"What pesticide did the lab find in the corn bread?"

"Furadan."

I stopped breathing for a moment. I thought of Juan Carlos's father in a cowboy hat.

"How could someone put Furadan in food without another person detecting it?"

"Furadan is colorless, odorless, and tasteless," Gina said. "And it doesn't take much to kill someone."

"But if the dose is small enough, it can just make you sick," Dorothy said. "You get dizzy, feel nauseous, maybe throw up. That's what saved Professor Elliott. But he seems to have had a heart attack too. Furadan affects the respiratory and nervous systems, so it's not clear what shape he'll be in if he does come out of the coma."

I was silent for a moment.

"What's happening with Juan Carlos Vega?" I asked, as casually as I could.

"He's still a person of interest, but we can't tell you more."

"When you came to see me the first time, I think you knew I was the one who made the corn bread. Why did you assume that? I don't think Frank noticed what anyone brought, and, as far as I know, no one else had identified the corn bread with me when you first asked him questions."

Dorothy looked down at the fake wood circle of the table.

"We can't tell you," she said.

Gluten-free Cornmeal Pancakes with Candied Kumquats

For ten 4" pancakes

Candied Kumquats

¼ cup coconut sugar
2 tablespoons honey
½ cup water
A dash of pure vanilla

extract
2 cups fresh kumquats,
washed, cut, and seeded

Cornmeal Pancakes

⅓ cup cornmeal
½ cup oats, ground into
flour
¼ teaspoon baking soda
½ teaspoon baking
powder
A pinch each of salt and
lemon zest

1 egg
½ cup almond milk
¼ teaspoon pure vanilla
extract
1 teaspoon honey
1 tablespoon melted coco-
nut oil

For the candied kumquats, heat the coconut sugar, honey, water, and vanilla extract in a small saucepan or a small skillet over medium-high heat until the sugar is dissolved and liquid begins to boil.

Add the kumquats, reduce the heat to medium, and cook uncovered for 10 to 12 minutes, until the kumquats soften.

Once they are cooked, remove the kumquats with a slotted spoon into a bowl and bring the liquid back to a boil over medium-high heat and reduce until syrupy. It should be thick enough to coat the back of the spoon. Transfer the syrup into a small bowl and set aside.

For the pancakes, whisk together the cornmeal, oat flour, baking soda and powder, salt, and lemon zest in a small mixing bowl.

Whisk together the egg, almond milk, vanilla, honey, and coconut oil in another small mixing bowl. Pour the milk mixture into the flour mixture and whisk until thoroughly combined.

Heat a frying pan over medium-high heat. Cook pancakes using about 2 tablespoons of batter per pancake. Flip when edges begin to look dry and a few bubbles surface.

Serve pancakes with candied kumquats, a drizzle of the coconut sugar syrup, and yogurt if desired.

Adapted by permission of Rachel Leung and Rachel Chew at
http://www.radiantrachels.com/
gluten-free-cornmeal-pancakes-with-candied-kumquats/.

Chapter 10

The sun brushed the sky with bands of rose and yellow, as I drove past the eastern edge of town to enter a subdivision that had opened in the 1960s. Houses in Los Campos de los Palominos, or Palomino Fields, cost more than those elsewhere—being surrounded by acres of untamed habitat and boasting a golf course said to be the best in town. The golf course sported a country club with a dining room as well, which, when dressed for evenings with crisp white cloths and linen napkins, served up nut-encrusted halibut and tender rib-eye steaks along with pleasing views of swelling greens and of the spacious homes that perched along their edge. A fountain splashing peacefully in a glimmering pond gave the course the aura of a sanctuary, a well-tended sanctuary for those who could afford to buy a stately home on an eight-thousand-square-foot lot.

Despite its landedness and luxury, however, Palomino Fields struck me as sterile and a bit forlorn. The sprawling houses, some with columned porticos, were meant to show well and impress, but they retained the regulated feel of products from a well-heeled factory, and as I continued down the wide, but mazelike, streets, I was struck by the rightness of this place for Lorna Vogle. For it was to Lorna's residence that I was headed this late fall afternoon. I had been summoned, along with the heads of American and ethnic studies, to a reception for the chairs and directors of what would soon become the Division of Humanities.

I wasn't required to attend, but, in a time of shrinking budgets, I owed it to my program to show some deference to a woman whose hands would rest upon the kingdom's purse. I also hoped to discover what Lorna's invitation really meant. Did it suggest that the women's, American, and ethnic studies programs would be allowed to join forces as a named unit within the new Division of Humanities? Or was it a sign that Women's Studies would soon disappear into the Department of English? I chose to focus on the former thought. It might be the only way to get through the evening.

Other colleagues were arriving, and the front door was ajar, so I stepped in. A small, unlived-in living room, like an old-fashioned parlor, opened to the right, where people had put their coats. I unbuttoned my jacket and laid it on a pile. Following the sound of conversation, I passed a stiff and formal dining room and then a kitchen, brilliant with stainless steel, which had been taken over by the caterers. The latter, of course, looked right at home in all that burnished glory, but did Vice Provost Vogle actually use this fancy kitchen? Knowing Lorna, I thought it might be more for show.

Just beyond the kitchen, the hall gave way to an enormous room where conversations had begun to hum, and where, I saw, as soon as I'd entered it, the house had greatest impact. Wide and high ceilinged, it formed a giant rectangle pierced on one side with sliders that overlooked a swimming pool outside. With a fire burning assertively in a marble fireplace at one end and a long table laden with hors d'oeuvres grandly presenting itself at the other, it felt like the hall of a country manor, built for large gatherings and for display.

"Emily," Lorna said, tilting her head in a birdlike way. "How good to see you." She was wearing a plain brown suit, but her poufy scarf, the color of a robin's breast, gave her look a bright and autumn leaf–like feel. Behind her, a vase of orange-red dahlias, perfectly matching the scarf, stood on a table next to the leaping fire. Lorna had an eye for detail. The fire matched too.

"Thanks for inviting me," I said. "Your great room is terrific."

"It is, isn't it? I've been waiting to get into Palomino Fields for quite a while. Well, make yourself at home. Have some food." Lorna flitted off to greet the next arrival.

I headed toward the table to examine the hors d'oeuvres. The platters, which the university's official catering service had supplied, were familiar from past occasions. Laid out with pre-cision on orange-red cloth napkins, they offered crudités, brie melted in a crust, mini quiches, potatoes stuffed with bacon, and blue corn blini with a curl of orange smoked salmon atop a dollop of sour cream. The blini were a new and elegant touch. They were the kind of thing Miriam might well have served in her New York living room. From Miriam, of course, they would have come from the heart, but where Lorna was con-cerned I wasn't so sure. I was inclined to think of them—as I often thought of Lorna's spiffy suits and flamboyant scarves—as gestures toward a cheerful sociability meant to obscure her less friendly and less visible endeavors.

"Emily, how are you?" It was the chair of the French Department and a friend of the Women's Studies program. She was French, a delicate woman with shiny dark eyes and a black velvet dress with colored beading—the very kind of dress that I myself would have liked to wear.

"You look lovely!" I could always trust French women to dress with elegance.

"Merci," she said, putting one of the blini onto a small plate and looking quickly around the room, her eyes coming to rest on Lorna. The latter was standing near the fireplace talking to the head of the English Department, a tired-looking man whose hound–dog face seemed to sag into his tweed jacket.

"I've been wanting to talk with you. I'm on the special

committee for reorganizing Letters and Sciences. We received Isobel's petition for the Haven Hall programs to become a separate division. I think we can offer a compromise, not a separate division but a named unit in Humanities, but there's a major problem." She glanced at Lorna and at the man I couldn't help thinking of as Hound Dog near the fire. "Lorna opposes it." She picked up a blini with one tiny hand and nibbled on it like a charming French mouse.

"Oh geez!" I said, the familiar flare of anger coursing through my upper body. "What is it with her anyway? We try to do something innovative and creative, and she tries to quash it. She really does want to merge us with large departments and see us disappear." Only fifteen minutes into the evening and, already, the future of our programs was careening out of our control.

"It's tied to the budget cuts, in part. I know she'd like to get rid of French too. We're small and vulnerable." She wiped her lips daintily as if grooming a set of silky whiskers.

"But French is a traditional department, so you have some protection."

"It's true, and, unlike the Haven Hall programs, we're not exactly challenging the status quo, at least most of my colleagues aren't."

"Thanks for telling me." I felt my anger vying awkwardly with incipient depression. "We'll try to make a run around her," I said.

"I'll do what I can do on the committee."

I felt grateful once again for the feminist network that operated quietly below the surface at Arbor State. Spread over dozens of programs and departments, its members kept in touch by e-mail, sometimes voted in a block on campus affairs, and occasionally met in person to discuss conditions for women on the campus. If only women like Lorna shared the values of this group. What would that be like?

Alma had arrived, and I went to join her, hoping for some solace.

"Do you think the rest of our group is going to come?" she said. Her hair was spikier than usual this evening with an extra coat of gel. Perhaps, given the ambiguous way we'd all been summoned, she was making a statement.

"Some of them hate to be commandeered to occasions like this, but I figure it's smarter politics to show up."

"I just learned that Lorna is standing in the way of our becoming a separate unit."

"Why am I not surprised? But why should she oppose it? What sense does that make?" Alma looked into her glass of wine. "She wants to get rid of us. We're like the scum on Indian Creek as far as she's concerned." This time, Alma took a big sip of her Cabernet. "But we can't give up. Who else is on the committee? Maybe we can have a word with those who might be sympathetic."

"I'll e-mail and find out. We'll have to work around her in every way we can." Above Alma's head I could see Lorna leaning toward the chair of English and he toward her. I hoped they weren't discussing Women's Studies. Hound Dog glanced in my direction, frowned, further creasing his already corrugated brow, then looked quickly away as if caught red-handed. Oh no, I thought, they *are* discussing Women's Studies or at least its director, which was me.

"How's Frank doing?" I asked Alma, trying to divert myself from the unsavory stew of my own emotions.

"The police haven't been back, according to Isobel, but he's still a suspect. He's writing a paper about it. Expect a lengthy e-mail."

"It's inconceivable that anyone would suspect Frank of attempted murder. They've questioned Juan Carlos Vega in Environmental Toxicology too."

"Oh sure. What would they do without a Mexican to

harass?" Alma paused for a moment, looked into her glass once more, and then straight at me. "*Mire*, the police, as usual, assume it was one of us who's guilty, that whoever tried to poison Peter disagreed with his corporate politics. But maybe the person who tried to poison him wasn't someone who disagreed with Peter. It could just as easily be someone who shared his corporate values but saw him as a rival. People who operate inside dog-eat-dog ethics often do each other in."

Collin Morehead's square face flashed briefly across my memory. I'd already made a note to think more about him. I wondered what Tess knew about her colleague, Collin.

"I need to think about that," I said, stealing a peek at Lorna and the chair of English, who were still absorbed in conversation. As the room had grown more crowded, they'd inched ever closer to the fire, keeping others away as if trying to conceal the topic of their talk. That didn't look good.

"I had another visit from the police," I said, determined to put a lid on my growing anxiety about Lorna and Hound Dog's secretive exchanges. "And what's really disturbing is that they seem to think someone is trying to throw suspicion on me. I've been getting phone calls in the middle of the night."

"I hope you told the police about that. It happened once to me. The police had me ask the phone company to direct late night calls to a religious hotline, and it stopped. There are a lot of disgruntled students out there, and whoever it was needed to be prayed at forcefully."

"I did tell them and they gave me the same advice, but I hadn't thought about its being a student." I felt appalled at that idea too. I glanced at Lorna and the chair of English once again only to see an ember fly over the top of the fire screen and land on Hound Dog's jacket, which began to smolder. I grabbed Alma's arm, then pointed at Hound Dog.

"His coat's on fire."

"Oh, *Dios*," she said.

Glasses in hand, the two of us dashed across the room.

"Your coat! Fire!" I splashed my glass of club soda toward his tailbone.

His droopy eyes went wide in horror as he turned to look at me and fell backward, colliding with Lorna.

"What in God's name," he sputtered as steam wafted from his jacket.

"Emily!" Lorna looked at me aghast, mouth open, eyes rounded.

"Fire! He's on fire!"

"What are you talking about?" Lorna said, angry at being interrupted and then trampled upon because of my seemingly deranged behavior.

At that moment, the chair of the French Department, who'd scurried across the room emitting small cries and waving one of the cloth napkins as if it were an orange NASCAR flag, began to beat it on the edge of Hound Dog's jacket, as if delivering a light spanking. The napkin, having served as resting place for the platter of blini, left streaks of salmon and cream cheese in its wake.

"Have you gone mad?" He was shouting now, his face aglow with heat and anger. In desperation, a meek-looking man, obviously following my example, gingerly tossed his half glass of brandy at the burning jacket.

"Not alcohol," I cried. "It's flammable!" A small blue flame flickered on Hound Dog's back as if warmed brandy had been poured into a pot of coq au vin.

A crowd had gathered, faces pale and shocked.

"Fire!"

"Oh, God!"

"Roll him on the floor!"

I picked up the vase and desperately tossed the water and flowers together at his back.

"Stop this, instantly!" he cried. His face was red with rage, and bits of dahlia clung to him as if he'd turned into a fall bouquet. Finally, Alma stepped up, hooked her hands on Hound Dog's front lapels, shook him, and spoke directly to his face. He was lucky she hadn't slapped him for good measure.

"Your coat is on fire. We are trying to put it out."

Finally, a look of comprehension dawned in his red-rimmed eyes.

"Fire?" he said at last, feeling the back of this jacket, which was now completely sodden.

"Fire?" Lorna said. Ophelia-like, her suit bore bits of dahlia too.

"I'm sorry," I said to Hound Dog, "I didn't want to see you burned." I hadn't wanted to see him burned, but was I entirely sorry about the vase of dahlias?

Lorna yanked Hound Dog's shoulders and turned him around to get a look at the damage. She took one sleeve and then another and pulled his flower-strewn jacket off. Then taking his arm in her right hand and his jacket in her left, she led him to the bathroom so he could work on his shirt and his composure. When she returned, her poufy orange scarf, which had suffered collateral damage from the water, had lost its plumpness. It looked less like a robin's breast now and more like a dead cowbird.

"I'll get the caterers," I said. They came, armed with towels and sponges, handed Lorna a towel, mopped up the floors near the fireplace—thank God, the floors were tile—and began restoring a sense of order to the table of hors d'oeuvres. The blini I had so admired, having toppled when the chair of French had grabbed the napkin from underneath their platter, lay in an orange, white, and blue-brown heap all over the floor. Too bad. They were made of corn and I hadn't had a chance to try them.

Lorna, after dabbing at her scarf and suit, put on a brave smile.

"Everything's fine," she said. "Please continue."

People returned to their conversations, and the party went on, though with greater liveliness than before because everyone now had an exciting topic of conversation. Alma and I returned to our spot near the door, my cheeks still burning from the debacle and from the looks of shock that had been directed at me. Well, that does it, I thought. Women's Studies will never be lodged in English. Suspicions about me and the poisoning and now the spectacle of my dousing the chair of the department with a vase of flowers and water surely made me and my program too much of a risk. Despite the fiasco that had just unfolded, I began to feel relief, until it occurred to me that Lorna might be more determined than ever to disappear me and the program into English just to bring us under control. The thought was crushing. I'd heard a lot about the department's gender wars.

I left soon after, making my goodbyes, thanking Lorna for her hospitality, and apologizing once again for the watery havoc. Though, really, shouldn't she be apologizing to me as well? She was gracious, if grateful to see me go. Lorna was adept at playing hostess, I mused, as I buttoned up my jacket. I had to admire her, and yet, this evening's event, like all her others, seemed mainly designed to buy goodwill while further disguising her secret attempts to do us in. What made her think we didn't know, or couldn't find out, what she was really up to? Was I missing something or were these sociable displays as manipulative as they seemed?

★ ★ ★

I opened the front door, and stepped into a cloud of white. The entire street had disappeared in a blanket of tule fog. It was early for the fog—it usually came in November—and my heart tumbled in my chest. I always got lost in it, even on familiar streets, and Palomino Fields was not familiar. Shaken by the imbroglio at Lorna's house, I climbed into my car, turned on the low beams, and tried to remember how I'd come. Ten minutes later, I found myself driving on the freeway, which I hadn't meant to do. The fog had blinded me and instead of going straight, I'd ended up on the highway, heading east. Oh hell, I thought. How did I do this? My night vision was poor as it was, and in this shrouding whiteness what little intuition for direction I possessed had been thrown entirely off.

When the fog thinned for an instant, revealing an exit sign, I got off and found the entrance for going west, but ten minutes later the cloud of fog grew dense and suddenly the road felt different beneath my tires. With a heart like desert rock, I sensed I was no longer on the freeway. I'd drifted onto an exit lane without knowing it and was driving on one of the country roads that divided large stretches of open field. Even by day these roads looked all the same and the tiny signs that marked them were hard to read. I had driven them only twice when the sun was shining, and now, in the milky mist, I felt at sea.

What if I couldn't find my way back? What would I do? In the snowy vapor I couldn't see if there were any houses on this road. I tried to calm myself by thinking that I could always pull over, lock all the doors, and stay in my car until the fog lifted, although the idea of sleeping in a car all night on a lonely country road did not appeal. I drove to the shoulder of the road to think, and then in the rearview mirror I saw a pair of headlights. Perhaps I can signal this driver and ask directions. I rolled down the window halfway and was poised to honk when a blue van drove slowly by in the white air. My throat closed up, and with a screech of tires I turned my car back onto the road and headed back in the direction from which I'd just come.

A vein throbbed in my neck as I drove into the ghostly bank ahead. I felt lost the way I'd felt as a child with absent parents. Despite my years of therapy, that lost little girl had a habit of reappearing in times of stress, and she was here now as I drove blindly down an unknown road. I really was lost, not just on this road but in my struggle to save the programs and in my efforts to separate myself and my colleagues from the poisoning. I thought of crying, but what good would crying do? It would only make me feel less powerful. Instead, I barreled on and on into the vaporous sea until, out of nowhere, a dimly lit green sign appeared barely visible in the mist—Arborville, 3 miles.

Relief drenched me. I had gotten back on the freeway as mysteriously as I had gotten off. Was it a matter of bad, and then good, luck? Was it a metaphor for how random one's life really was, for how small one was in the midst of massive forces? Or was finding my way again a sign of greater clarity to come? My attempts so far to unravel the mystery of Peter's poisoning had gotten nowhere and now I was falling apart every time I saw a blue van. The poisoning had hijacked my life. I needed answers soon. Maybe my colleagues, with whom I was dining the following evening, might have some new ideas. I desperately hoped the phone would not disturb my rest again that night.

But at 3:00 a.m., its ringing jolted me from sleep with the force of a skidding car. I decided not to answer it but lay there for an hour while the throbbing of my heart slowly subsided.

★ ★ ★

La Salvia Bianca, which meant white sage in Italian, was a low, white stucco building with a red tile roof and a portico in front sustained by a series of brown posts. A large courtyard across from the entrance held tables and umbrellas, and in summer it was further shaded by large trees. Two terracotta fountains bubbled in the middle of the courtyard, and long strings of lights outlined and crisscrossed the square. The place was magical on a warm summer's evening. I remembered how I'd dined with my Women's Studies colleagues last June, before I'd become a suspect in a case of attempted murder, before I'd gotten calls in the middle of the night. I'd been carefree then. Now I was full of troubles, and October had given a bite to the evening air. I looked forward to seeing the faces of my friends.

Every now and then, I and some of my Women's Studies colleagues went out to dinner for the pure pleasure of being together—away from the university and from the program's struggles to maintain itself during the repeated cuts. It restored us, and we were lucky that we enjoyed each other's company. Not all women's studies programs were so fortunate, and even our own had a new hire who was troubling the waters. Fortunately, she was good at getting grants and was away for the entire quarter.

Tonight a group of us had decided to treat ourselves by going to our favorite restaurant, one of the few places in town that still had tablecloths and candles. It was quiet and there was a table that seated six. The inside of the restaurant had a nineteenth-century European feel. In the candlelight one could just see that the walls were painted red. Red, hand-embroidered drapes framed the windows, and on every table a slender vase held a single flower, this night a spiky white chrysanthemum. I seated myself in the middle of the long table, with my back comfortably to the wall, and awaited my colleagues. La Salvia Bianca was expensive, but its soothing warmth and richness were just what I needed after the disastrous evening at Lorna's the night before and then my hour of driving, lost and frightened, in the fog. La Salvia Bianca reminded me of a restaurant Miriam and I had once visited.

Ursula Romanoff, my most candid colleague, arrived first.

"Em-i-ly!" Ursula had slid over from the Russian department several years ago.

A woman with beautifully coifed blonde hair, she dressed herself like a piece of modern art—black tights, a long red sweater, yellow earrings and a matching clunky necklace. How does she do that? I wondered. I often felt barely pulled together. Helena and Grace came next along with Callie Jones, my newest colleague, a young woman with a face as fresh and as open as that of a brown gerbera daisy. We took turns hugging hello. They were like family and I could feel myself unwinding.

"What are you having?" Ursula inquired.

"The usual."

"Me too." We both ordered the lamb shank with garlic roasted potatoes and a house salad that came encased in an edible parmesan bowl. Ursula ordered a bottle of pinot noir for the table, and we settled in.

"I have a question for you," I said. "You've all heard about my corn bread being involved in the attempted murder."

"Who hasn't?" Ursula said.

It was true that news of my unfortunate baking project was now known all over campus.

"The first time the police came to me, I think they knew I was the one who made the corn bread? How would they have known that?"

"Would Frank have told them?" Grace asked.

"He didn't know who made the corn bread. I don't think anyone at the reception really noticed what anyone brought. We just put our dishes on a table."

Callie wrinkled her forehead, half closing her large, fawn-like eyes. Helena moved her knife closer to the spoon as if rearranging the silverware might realign her thoughts.

"I don't think that's a question we can answer," Ursula replied. "What else have you got?"

"The police came to question me for a second time and to tell me that the ingredients the lab found in the piece of corn bread were the same ingredients I'd use in my special recipe. The one with caramelized onion and goat cheese."

"Gee," said Callie, "I make that corn bread too. Remember, you gave me the recipe last spring." Callie and I shared an interest in food.

"I'd forgotten that." I paused to consider. "So this recipe is in greater circulation than I thought. Okay, then there's even more of a puzzle." I pushed my limp hair behind my ears in an effort to somehow clarify the situation. Callie was lucky. She could wear her hair cut close to her scalp and it only made her eyes look more dramatic.

The server delivered warm bread and parsley oil for dipping.

"There are some other things," I continued. "Everyone who's been questioned was at the panel on GMOs and three of us were also at the reception. And the suspects are either feminist women or men of color."

"The usual suspects," Ursula said. She dipped a piece of bread in the fragrant oil. "My God this oil is great!"

Several others began tearing and dipping their bread as well.

"But I don't think these police take that attitude. The officers who questioned me were a black woman and a Latina."

"Let's think this through," Helena said. She took out a small pad of paper from her purse. "Okay, four people we know of were questioned: Frank Walker, Juan Carlos Vega, Tess Ryan, and you. Three of you were at both the panel and the reception, and Tess was on the panel. Three on the panel publically disagreed with Peter about corporate patents. And those three were questioned. Who would have told the police about the panel?"

"Anyone who was there of course or anyone close to Peter, like his wife, someone he would confide in," Callie said. Callie always had some insight about relationships. Although she and I were many years apart in age, we'd become girlfriends, talking with and e-mailing each other about our experiences with men. We'd both been looking for a partner.

"Look," Ursula sopped up more of the green-flecked oil, "someone close to Peter may have suggested names to the police, but what does that prove? It doesn't mean the person gave him poisoned corn bread."

"That's true," I said. "Maybe there's no point in trying to figure out what logic the police are pursuing. Let's try to figure out who had a motive."

The server delivered salads.

"I wonder if the police have cleared Peter's wife," I said. "She'd have a motive from everything I understand about Peter, and what if she had someone working with her?" I thought about Juan Carlos's blush. I didn't want to suspect Juan Carlos, a man from my own hometown, a man who belonged to the network of my Native American and Chicana/o Studies colleagues, a man whose philosophy of life would appear to rule out harming another being, but still I didn't want to be naïve.

"A lover might have had a motive," Helena said. Grace and I exchanged glances. I knew better than to mention Mei Lee.

"There's a graduate student, Jenny Archer," I said. "He might have been involved with her. She might have known about the panel. She might have attended the panel too, although I didn't know her then and don't remember."

"Look her up." Ursula shrugged her shoulders. "What've you got to lose?"

"There's also Save the Fields," Helena added. "They've been active. Someone followed Tess home two weeks ago, and today there was a bomb threat directed at a lab."

"Tess told me they drove a dark blue van. I've been running into that van or into vans that look a lot like it. It's really putting me on edge."

"Emily, this is a family town. There are lots and lots of vans, many of them dark blue," Ursula reminded me.

"That's true too." Ursula's common sense grounded me. The server had arrived with our dishes. Ursula cut into her lamb with a decisive motion, and I pulled at mine with a fork. The lamb was tender and falling off the bone. For a while, the only sounds were those of eating and drinking. The tender lamb, and garlicky potatoes, the mellow pinot noir—this was California after all—and the reassuring sounds of my colleagues eating their cioppino and seafood lasagna soothed me, softening the memories of Lorna's maneuvering, my farce with the flower vase, and then my helplessness in the fog.

During dinner we discussed Lorna's resistance to the proposed union of the five programs.

"Being united would mean so much to us as a community," Grace said. "It's not just a matter of being strong. We'd draw closer to each other. It would enrich our lives." Grace was always alert to ways of caring for others. It was a way of being she carried on in other parts of her existence. When I had first visited her small home on the greenbelt, I had observed five cats, two perched on counters, three curled up on a sofa. Over time, the number of cats had increased exponentially, as Grace became more deeply involved in a network of women who rescued cats and kittens from bad owners and painful circumstances. Grace frequently offered her most special cats to me, but Sadie, who'd had a bad experience with a calico while only a puppy, would never have stood for sharing quarters with a feline.

It was only after we'd finished our entrees and were contemplating dessert, that I described my encounter with Ned Goldman, the butterfly man. "I actually thought he might have been the one the police were searching for, and maybe he was. Maybe the police and I both assumed that Ned was a member of Save the Fields, though now that I think about it, I'm sure vandals don't look so obvious."

"No," Grace said. "There's an old saying, 'the sea can't be measured with a bucket.'"

"Ned Goldman," Helena said, "is not likely to have poisoned anyone, though did you know that Furadan, the poison the police now say they found, is suspected of interrupting the life cycle of monarch butterflies? Ned's an expert on monarchs."

There were still way too many threads, but having dinner

with my colleagues had given me energy and new direction. I would investigate Collin Morehead, but I would also find out more about the women in Peter's life.

Blue Corn Blini with Smoked Salmon

Makes 4 servings.

Blini

3 tablespoons milk, lightly
heated
1 package active dried
yeast
2 teaspoons sugar
¼ cup unbleached all-
purpose flour

¼ cup blue cornmeal
1 egg yolk
6 tablespoons (¾ stick)
unsalted butter
2 egg whites
¼ teaspoon cream of tartar

Sauce

¾ cup sour cream
¼ cup mild goat cheese,
room temperature,
crumbled
1 jalapeño chile, finely

minced
¼ teaspoon ground white
pepper
1½ teaspoons lime juice

Accompaniments

1 red bell pepper, roasted,
peeled, seeded, and cut
into a ¼-inch dice

1 yellow bell pepper,
roasted, peeled, seeded,
and cut into a ¼-inch
dice

¼ cup red onion, finely
diced
2 tablespoons chopped
fresh cilantro

2 tablespoons fresh chives,
sliced
½ pound thinly sliced
smoked salmon

For the blini:

In a medium bowl, combine the milk, yeast, and sugar. Stir the mixture well and allow it to develop at room temperature until foamy, about 10 to 15 minutes.

Whisk in the flour and blue cornmeal, mixing until no lumps remain. Set aside.

Whip the egg yolk and 2 tablespoons of the butter together with an electric beater until the mixture is light and fluffy. Add the yeast mixture and continue to beat until the batter does not cling to the beaters, about 10 minutes.

In another bowl, whip the egg whites with an electric beater until foamy. Add the cream of tartar and then beat on high speed until the egg whites are stiff.

Fold 1/3 of the egg whites gently into the blue corn batter to lighten and then gently fold in the rest. Set the batter aside, keeping it at room temperature.

For the sauce:

In a small bowl, mix the sour cream, goat cheese, jalapeño chile, lime juice, and white pepper. Refrigerate the sauce until ready to serve.

Frying the blini:

Melt one tablespoon of butter in a small nonstick skillet over medium-high heat. When the butter foam begins to subside, add ¼ of the batter and fry the blini until golden, about 2 minutes.

Turn and cook for an additional 2 minutes. Transfer the blini to a plate with a spatula and keep warm in a 150°F oven while making the remaining blini.

To serve:

Place one blini in the center of a plate. Sprinkle with ¼ of the red and yellow peppers, onion, cilantro, and chives.

Form the smoked salmon into a rose-shaped cup in the center of the blini by rolling it into a spiral (it doesn't have to be perfect). Fill the rose with ¼ of the sour cream and quickly repeat with the remaining ingredients. Serve immediately.

Adapted by permission of Taralee Lathrop at My Kitchen Ink
http://www.mykitchenink.com/recipes/auth_1/recipe/75/.

Chapter 11

I studied the campus map, wondering how I could meet up with Peter's graduate student Jenny Archer. Graduate students weren't that easy to track down. For one thing, students in Plant Biology spent long hours in the lab, and I felt reluctant to intrude in someone's work space, even if this was a case of attempted murder. But graduate students had to eat lunch like everybody else. I hoped that Jenny wasn't the type to bring a brown bag lunch and consume it in an office. The Plant Biology labs, according to the map, weren't far from the Granary, a building that housed a collection of fast-food vendors, a coffee café, and a mini mart with the usual university fare. Perhaps I could take my article on shrimp and grits and work at one of the outdoor tables that were pleasingly shaded by surrounding trees.

I wouldn't be wasting my time but putting it to double purpose, revising the essay and looking out for Jenny. Walking from my usual parking lot to the Granary would also count as part of my exercise that day. More than ever, I realized, I was multitasking. Trying to solve a mystery on top of reading, preparing classes, teaching, writing, publishing, directing the program, writing documents, serving on committees, attending campus meetings, and tending to Polly, not to mention pursuing a new relationship with Wilmer Crane—all of this required ever more skills in time management. I thought again about the woman with eight arms on the cover of *Ms. Magazine*. At least I wasn't pregnant.

I collected my materials and drove to campus, arriving at the Granary a little before noon and finding a shaded table that had a good view of the back door. Flows of faculty and students poured in and out, the largely male faculty in science easily identified by their uniform of striped, plaid, or polo shirts; jeans or chinos; and sneakers or sensible brown walking shoes. I took the top off the tuna salad I had purchased and began to eat. After twenty minutes, I'd finished my salad and had made some headway on revisions when Jenny Archer walked out the Granary's back door. Tables were emptying by now, and Jenny found a table for herself next to the building. I threw my plastic box and fork into a recycling bin, gathered up my papers as if I were about to leave, and walked in the direction of Jenny's table. I saw that she had bought herself two hard-boiled eggs and a bottle of water.

"Jenny?"

She looked at me with a puzzled air.

"I'm Emily Addams. I attended the meeting about the grant for women in science and heard you speak. I was interested in what you said. Would you mind if I asked you some questions?"

Jenny's tight face loosened.

"Sure. Have a seat."

"I was concerned when you said that a professor had passed off your work as his. You don't have to tell me details about your situation, if you don't want to, but I wondered if you could tell me, generally, how this kind of thing gets done." I hadn't noticed before how thin Jenny was. She had hollows in her cheeks, and her arms seemed bony. The veins stood out on them like tiny ropes. Does she have an eating issue? I wondered, looking at the two boiled eggs.

"I'm afraid it goes on all over the country. You work in your professor's lab on a project that he's designed. You develop some compound or isolate some gene or make some innovation in technology on your own, and before you know it, he's published it in a paper that, maybe, thanks you but doesn't give you coauthorship." Jenny cracked one of her eggs with a thwack on the edge of the table. "It's a slave system. What you produce goes to the master. I wouldn't mind his putting his name on my work if he would just give me proper credit. Graduate students have to publish to get jobs."

"That's terrible." Never having given a thought to graduate work in the sciences, I was taken aback. "Is there anyone you can complain to?"

"Officially." Jenny began to peel the egg, leaving the shells on a napkin she had spread neatly before her. "But I have very little money. I've borrowed to get through and I depend on my lab salary, which my professor pays. If I complained to him, he wouldn't reappoint me and I'd be sunk. It would hurt my chance to be hired in another lab too." Jenny's gray eyes had taken on a haunted look. "And, anyway, he's my major professor. I'm going to need his recommendation and connections to get a job after I finish. He's on my dissertation committee too, and I'm almost near the end. I can't afford to make him angry, though now, of course, he's in a coma so I don't know what will happen."

"It's Peter Elliott, I assume."

Jenny nodded and bit into her egg.

"Is there anyone you could talk to who might have influence?"

"The people with influence have worked with Peter for years. They aren't going to take my side. Besides, it's a way of life in his lab. A lot of people know about it, and they just let it go on. Please don't tell anyone what I've said." Her brown hair was pulled so tightly in her ponytail that the skin along the sides of her face looked taut. Graduate student life had thinned and sharpened her like the edge of an arrowhead.

"One word from Peter could ruin my career. And before the poisoning he'd gotten irritable." Jenny folded the napkin with the eggshells into a small neat square.

"What do you think that was about?" I asked.

"I'm not sure. He'd gotten paranoid about his notes. He made sure we all locked up our own."

"Would it have been the vandalism that made him so concerned?" I remembered how Tess had reacted to Save the Field's threats.

"That didn't help." Jenny folded the napkin into a smaller square. "But Peter had grown uneasy before that. For all his faults, he used to be kind of jovial. He'd joke about things. But that stopped this summer."

I wondered what had happened to Peter before Save the Fields had torn up the cornfield. I felt for Jenny. Graduate student life was looking rough, but, at the same time, I wondered how deep her relationship with Peter Elliott had gone. I also wanted desperately to ask her if she baked. I told her I was sorry and that I hoped we could address situations like hers in the grant. Her face lit up for a moment and then the moment passed.

"I admired Peter at first because his labs get good results, and he's always funded. I thought I'd found a kind of home. But it became more like a plantation. He just assumed everything belonged to him. Once, as I was eating lunch in my office, he came in to tell me something and helped himself to one of my boiled eggs without even asking. I don't even know if he was conscious that it wasn't his."

A thin young man with a well-trimmed beard walked up to the table.

"This is my friend, Kevin," Jenny said. "Kevin, this is Professor Addams."

I said it was nice to meet him. He too was thin as an insect, a tall praying mantis.

"Jenny, if I can do anything for you, please let me know. I'll be sure to bring this up in the grant meetings, but without using your name of course."

"Thanks," Jenny said, tucking the other egg into her purse. "I have to get back."

She and Kevin left the table and walked away. They were the skinniest young people I'd ever seen. I wondered if they ate boiled eggs for dinner. It was doubtful that Jenny dined on corn bread, although given the grazing habits of her major professor, a napkin full of poisoned corn bread might be the perfect vehicle of revenge. I was aware, of course, that poisoning one's major professor would not contribute much to finishing one's degree, but I surmised that if Peter were to die or linger in his coma, Jenny would be assigned a new adviser. Maybe she'd get lucky. Maybe a different professor would let her keep her name on her own work. And what of her personal relationship to Peter? If they'd been involved, and knowing Peter, perhaps unsatisfactorily involved, how would that have figured in? And, finally, the detail about Peter's notes. I wondered what had caused him to become so guarded. Perhaps it was Peter's agitation about his work that Mei Lee had sensed and misidentified as a loss of interest in their relationship. These bits of information were tantalizing.

★ ★ ★

The administration building, Murk Hall, had been built in the 1960s, a five-story building with slit-like windows that vaguely recalled the computer punch cards of that era. It had been named after a previous chancellor, but folk legend had it that the construction workers had decided to call it Murk after Indian Creek, which sometimes filled with algae, giving the waters an opaque and greenish look. Murk was the site of many committee meetings, which, God knows, had their own elements of dreck and nontransparency, and I was headed to still another, this one called by the Office of Research—a powerful operation. Responsible for supporting and organizing academic investigations on campus, it had secured $340,000,000 in funds the previous year. Now, twenty-seven units reported to the office—exactly twenty-six on science and one on women and gender. Given the differences in the way scientific and nonscientific research were defined, it was a troubled marriage. The head of the research center on women and gender, a Women's Studies colleague of mine, an anthropologist who worked on a lesser-known Chinese ethnic group, had a conference that day and had asked me to go in her place. I wasn't keen on attending another meeting, but, of course, I couldn't say no.

As I entered the meeting room, the atmosphere was somber. The latest budget crisis was so severe that it was threatening to have impact not just on the women and gender unit, but on the scientific ones as well. The director of the office, a blond out of an ad for Ralph Lauren, wore a well-tailored navy suit and tie which would have looked at home in a board room. His lustrous black shoes appeared soft and possibly Italian. I wondered what kind of salary he was paid.

"We're facing another series of budget cuts and every unit is being asked to contribute. How should we respond?" The director looked at us blandly, as if he didn't already know the answer.

"We can't take any cuts," Collin Morehead barked. As in the Super Committee meeting, the extra folds around his mouth gave his jaws a massive, Cerberus-like look. "We don't have enough funding as it is to do our work."

I remembered how Collin had taken the corporate line at the GMO panel along with Peter, and I also remembered that they had not appeared to be too friendly. Like Peter, he also worked on corn. Could Collin and Peter be rivals? I remembered Alma's comment about those who espoused dog-eat-dog values.

"What are our options?" the director asked smoothly. He wasn't anticipating answers that might challenge the way things were. I sensed instantly that the center for women and gender was going to take a hit.

How about lowering the salary of the director of the Office of Research? I thought. How about lowering all the other bloated salaries and privileges of the administration? What would he do if I had said that out loud? The argument that obscenely large salaries were necessary to get good people from afar was a complete fabrication in my opinion. People from inside the university were often better at administrative jobs than those brought to the campus at great expense. People from inside knew the culture, and knowing the culture and the people counted. They'd seen the track records of the departments in terms of service, mentoring students, and intellectual vibrancy. They knew the quality of small programs and of the people who made them work. People from outside lacked that knowledge, and the swollen salaries often brought in people who conflated "big" with "good" and were likely to identify productivity with numbers.

But I couldn't speak up and risk hurting my colleague's center any more than it was already going to be. The center on women and gender was already regarded as an exotic effluence among the scientific units.

"Shall we propose to raise student tuition instead?"

The director's suggestion was met with a hum of agreement.

"We can also propose a cut in staff," Collin growled with perfect confidence that his suggestion would be well received.

Another approving hum confirmed that his confidence was not misplaced. I was boiling. Oh sure, I thought, send the staff packing despite their years of loyalty and double the workload of the lowest-paid employees—people, for the most part, who are already overworked, underpaid, and raising families. I scribbled on my notepad to cool my outrage. The privilege of many of my colleagues, their lack of attention to anything but their own work, their failure to see how their own projects were in fact sustained by the very staff they saw no issue in further burdening roiled my insides. I thought of Peter's staff person, Yvonne, who was struggling to support three children and an aging mother on her own, and the words shot out.

"Staff are already overburdened. We can't just keep taking from those who support our work and make so little. It's shameful and counterproductive. We should be cutting our own salaries, especially those at the top."

A man with a beard and two women looked at me with sympathy, but, for the most part, my remarks slipped by as if they had fallen into a large, quiet sea. I wished the bearded man would speak. Men often listened to other men, even when they espoused the same opinion as a woman whom they'd previously ignored. Many in the room understood ecology in respect to the natural world, but when it came to the interdependence of the human world, some appeared not to have a clue.

"I think I have a sense of your feelings about this," the director said, as he brought the meeting to a close.

He didn't mean my feelings, of course, or those of the few who'd given me a friendly look. More and more, an emerging culture was encouraging people to only care about their own interests. This was true even in women's and in ethnic studies. As Alma and Grace both had complained, older faculty had made it possible for the younger ones to enter the university in the first place, but the culture of struggle and community that had won the young their places now seemed irrelevant to some.

After the meeting ended, I left the room and decided to take the wide marble stairs. I was in no mood to be enclosed in an elevator with my colleagues from the meeting. On the stairs, I was joined by the man with the beard.

"Quite a show in there," he said.

"Do you mean how they all jumped to cut staff and raise tuition for the students and ignored my suggestion about cutting salaries at the top?"

"It's the corporate model. They justify those salaries just the way Wall Street does. It's a bunch of bull. But if you're an academic in the sciences, now, given all the cuts in state and federal funding, you're so hungry for money that you're liable to be working with a corporation and attending to its interests." Despite the beard, he had an open, friendly face with spokes of laugh lines at the corner of his eyes.

"How bad is it?" Doing analysis of popular culture, as I did, did not require equipment or a lab.

"Well," he frowned, "nationally, biotech conglomerates are asking many of the questions. Taxpayer monies buy the labs and equipment, the conglomerates pay for some of the research, and then they try to patent the professor's discoveries and take most of the profit. Universities can patent discoveries too— Arbor State insists on it—but corporations own most of the new technologies."

"Has it changed the way you work? By the way, what do you work on?"

"I study the environmental effects of biotechnology, which the big bio tech companies aren't interested in funding."

We'd reached the bottom of the stairs and were headed toward the front door.

"It would cut into their profits?" I asked.

"Exactly. Companies don't pay for research that's not in their own interest. They don't make money on risk assessment. They do make it on biotechnology." We opened the wide doors and left the building but lingered on the front steps, neither of us ready to end the conversation.

"Research used to feel collaborative," he said, taking off his glasses and cleaning them with a handkerchief from his pants pocket. "You'd talk to your colleagues about your work and kind of share ideas. But now that some researchers are hooked up with corporations, they're afraid to share what they're thinking about. I've known a few on other campuses who keep their notebooks locked up. Sometimes they have stock in corporations." He held his glasses up to check for spots and then put them carefully back in place.

"Do you know Peter Elliott?"

His face took on a look of disgust.

"Yeah, I know him."

"Is he an aberration or is he the future?"

"God, I hope he's not the future. He's practically a lobbyist for Syndicon. I mean, given cuts in public funding, we're all hungry for money to sustain our work. I know a guy who'd been approached by a company to do research and to turn over all discoveries to them, for a price. He would have been working for the corporation. Fortunately, the chair of his department wouldn't let him go that far. We're supposed to be finding new knowledge and technologies that will benefit the public."

"I'm in Women's Studies, by the way. I'm glad we had this talk."

"Plant Sciences. Thanks for listening."

★ ★ ★

I'd had enough of meetings for the day and decided on a greenbelt walk, although my amble, I had already determined, would serve a dual purpose. It would help me shake off my anger at the wrongheadedness I'd just witnessed at the meeting, and it would serve to further my investigation of Peter's poisoning. I'd looked up Peter Elliott's address and realized that he, too, lived off the greenbelt but over by the pond. I could easily arrange to pass right by his house at 30 Wild Deer Lane, and it occurred to me that I might knock on Peter's door and have a chat with Peter's wife. I'd introduce myself as a neighbor and as the colleague who might have baked the fatal corn bread and ask about Peter's health and see where that would lead. It was potentially embarrassing, and I wanted to avoid another awkward conversation like the one with Juan Carlos Vega, but I was so deeply immersed in the seeping effect of Peter's poisoning that I was determined to give it a try.

I set off along the greenbelt, walking along a path that ran northward to some open fields, then along the fields to the west, and south again to the side of a small pond. Wild Deer Lane ended in a cul-de-sac that opened onto the greenbelt path and number 30 turned out to be the house at the very end, one that I had often admired. It was made of a soft, peach-colored stone and had a Southwestern feel. Its upper windows looked onto the trees bordering the pond. I climbed its three stone stairs and rang the bell. The heavy wooden door opened, and Teresa Fuentes-Elliott appeared wearing a white sweat suit with a folded red bandanna holding back her rich brown hair. She was prettier in person than in her website photo.

"Yes?" she said in slightly accented English.

"Professor Fuentes-Elliott?" Teresa nodded. "I'm one of your colleagues, Emily Addams. I live nearby and thought I'd ring your bell since I was walking right past your home. I was the one who baked the corn bread found in your husband's hand." Talk about awkward conversations, but there was nothing to do, so I rambled on. "At least, it seems to have been my corn bread. I'm very sorry about Peter, and I just wanted to let you know that I ate that corn bread and so did one of my colleagues, and we didn't get sick. Someone must have put something in the corn bread after I left it in Bauman Hall."

Teresa frowned slightly and crossed her arms.

"I wanted to offer my best wishes for Peter and maybe talk to you about who might have had access to the corn bread. I served it the night of the Native American reception in Bauman Hall. I'm a suspect in the case, and so are some of my colleagues." I was relieved to be getting through those initial mouthfuls. "I'm anxious to do what I can to figure out what happened that evening."

"I've been cleared by the police. I was at home all evening with my sister who'd come to visit. And there are no pesticides on the property. I'm a toxicologist, so I wouldn't allow them." She held her arms more tightly. Not exactly a good beginning.

"Yes, I assumed you'd been cleared. I wouldn't have come to accuse you. I just thought that, between us, we might be able to come up with some leads or clues. The corn bread was a special kind with caramelized onions and goat cheese. The police lab verified those ingredients."

Teresa looked a shade friendlier. "Okay, come in."

I entered the large foyer that looked out on the other end to the middle of the trees.

"Would you like some coffee?"

"I'd love some."

Teresa led me through a large dining room containing a rustic dark brown table, large enough for twelve. It had a view of the pond, and a bronze vase on its surface held a mass of deep yellow roses.

"What a wonderful dining room. I love the table."

"It's Colombian. That's where I'm from." We entered the kitchen, which was open and light with Spanish-looking pavers on the floor and counters.

"This is a beautiful kitchen. Do you do a lot of cooking?"

"I used to. Peter likes to entertain, and when we first moved here and got this house, we gave a lot of large dinner parties."

"I write on food now, and cooking is one of my passions. What kind of cooking do you do?"

Teresa stopped frowning.

"Colombian. *Empanadas,* of course, *patacones* or twice-fried plantains; *Ajiaco,* a chicken, corn, and potato stew; and *Bandeja Paisa* with steak, chorizo, *chicharon*—do you know *chicharon*?"

"Deep-fried bacon?"

"Yes, and fried egg, fried plantain, a little salad, and some rice."

"Wow, the *Bandeja* is a lot of food."

Teresa's full mouth curved slightly in something that could have passed for a smile.

"It's Peter's favorite. Colombians make corn bread too. *Arepas* are little corn cakes made from *masarepa* flour. You cook them in a broiler or on a grill until they have a nice crust. Then you eat them with more butter and sometimes cream cheese. I wish I had some right now."

Teresa's face relaxed even more as she poured coffee into two deep green mugs. "Sugar? Cream?"

"Both, please. How is Peter?"

"He's stable. His signs are good, but he hasn't come out of the coma. He had some heart trouble and the poison brought on a heart attack." Teresa looked down at the emerald-green mugs. "It's hard to be in this house alone. He took up a lot of space."

"Peter seems to have enjoyed good food," I observed and then stopped. Perhaps, in the context of the poisoning, it was indelicate to be discussing Peter's eating habits.

"Peter would eat anything I put on his plate. He'd eat off my plate too and drink my wine at the dinner table. He had few boundaries where food was concerned." Teresa handed me my mug. "His father was a poor pig farmer. I think Peter was deeply influenced by his childhood poverty—and by those hogs."

"Well, he made them a subject of his work, and, from what I can tell, he made it pay."

"Yes, Peter did far better with his swine than his father. Living on that pig farm was a hard life." Teresa looked out the window to the street. "Let's go into the living room to drink."

Teresa guided me back through the hall into the bright living room, which was furnished with leather couches and a large rustic coffee table. Some terra-cotta figurines in bright colors of red, white, and yellow lined the mantel of the fireplace.

"Do you have children?" I asked, sipping my coffee. Now that we were both sitting on the couch I could smell Teresa's perfume. Being allergic to scent, I never wore it myself, but Teresa's fragrance reminded me of blackberries and plums, of roses and orchids, and of something earthy and wood-like all in one. It suited Teresa who was far more glamorous than a toxicologist ought to be. She reminded me of something. What was it? A harvest? A flower market? Fruits spilling from a horn? Did she remind me of Miriam?

"Peter has three children from a former marriage, all grown. I met him when I was a graduate student. He was married then but left his wife, and when we married I was beginning a career, so stepchildren were enough." Teresa gathered her thick hair in her hands and gave it a twist. What would it be like, I wondered, to have hair so full and luxurious?

"You met in his lab?"

"Yes, Peter was always well funded and he was already a rising star. Getting into his lab was very competitive. I admired him. We fell in love."

"Sounds romantic." I took another sip of the coffee—sweet with a nutty undertone.

"Yes, until he met the next woman in his life." Teresa lowered her glance to the large wooden coffee table. "I'm sorry. But everyone knows about Peter's infidelities. They're legendary. I tried couples therapy with him, but nothing changed. He just assumes he has the right."

Like helping himself to Jenny's egg, I thought, like drinking Teresa's wine. And then to be poisoned by a piece of corn bread. Perhaps it, too, belonged to someone else? I took a long, thoughtful sip from my mug.

We sat in silence for a moment. It was interesting how often people were inclined to tell me things. Women in Chicana/o

Studies frequently came to me to discuss departmental conflicts. I was a neutral party, and they could count on my being empathetic. I was also a good listener. But Teresa had been especially frank, a characteristic, it would seem, of an expansive nature, and her openness had given her words an aura of authenticity. I felt emboldened to ask more questions.

"Did any of his, ah, women friends bake?"

"I've no idea. I stopped cooking for him long ago." She looked into her mug and then set it on the coffee table. "I came up for tenure just last year and before that I'd had to put every minute into my research. It got so we hardly saw each other much, and he often stayed on the couch in his office when he was working late."

"So you went your own way?"

"Yes, and he went his. I don't agree with his lobbying for Syndicon, which makes pesticides. And do we know that Peter's insect- and disease-resistant corn is safe? There's no money for studying the effects of products like that."

"But you continue on with Peter," I began but stopped. Was I pressing too far? Teresa's cheeks flushed.

"I had to work on tenure. There was no time to sort things out. When you're in science, the work shapes your life. At certain periods it just takes over. I don't know how women with young children do it at all." She picked up her mug again and cradled it in her long, slender hand.

"Do you think Peter was concerned about Save the Field's threats?" I remembered Jenny's comments about Peter's uneasiness.

"He was concerned about something, I know that. But it started well before they tore up the cornfield in September. This summer, he began to act funny. Sometimes I'd come into a room, and he'd close the cover of his laptop. At first I thought he was hiding e-mails from one of his amours, but then there would be times that we'd be driving somewhere together and he'd wonder if we were being followed." She gazed into the large, stone fireplace.

"Could one of his women friends have been jealous, do you think, or felt spurned?"

"Maybe, but there was something about his work that he was hiding. Ordinarily, he talked about his results. Then he stopped."

"I know there are a lot of people who disagreed with Peter, but it's hard to believe that the official suspects in the case would poison him for his views. Was he on bad terms with anyone else you knew?"

Teresa stared hard into the fireplace. I glanced at the picture over the mantel. It showed a lush valley with palm trees in the foreground and mountains half misted over in the back. I assumed it was Colombia. Did it smell like Teresa's scent?

"There was someone who saw himself as Peter's competition, Collin Morehead, who also works on genetically engineered corn. Syndicon gave Peter a big contract. Collin had wanted one but didn't manage to get it."

"Collin Morehead. I just attended a meeting with him. Do you know him?"

"Not well, but someone in Plant Biology would. He lives in Summerton."

Tess, I thought, but Tess was away. I decided to get in touch with Donna DeLacey, the editor of the *Summerton Post*. Donna knew everyone in town.

"Is that a picture of Colombia?" I asked, pointing at the painting.

"Yes, it's the Paisa district where I grew up. My father had a small coffee plantation in what's called the coffee triangle, where most of Colombia's coffee is grown. It's where I learned to care about what's on our food because coffee fields are thick with pesticide." The frown was back.

A phone rang in the hall. "Excuse me a minute," Teresa said

and disappeared. At a distance, I could hear her speaking in rapid Spanish.

"*Hola mi amor, no puedo hablar ahora. La mujer de quién me hablaste está aquí ahora. Te lo contare más tarde. ¿Okay? Realmente no puedo hablar.*"

When Teresa returned, I stood up to go. I thanked her for talking with me and said I hoped Peter got better. I liked her, a woman who spoke so openly, a woman with an appreciation for cooking, rustic tables, and yellow roses. Teresa walked me to the door and said goodbye. I descended the steps and turned back to the greenbelt. "*My love, I can't talk now. The woman you told me about is here. I'll tell you about it later. Okay? Really I can't talk.*" Teresa had assumed that I didn't understand the language, but raised in Southern California, I had been learning, and relearning, Spanish for most of my life. "The woman you told me about" could only be me—which meant that Teresa's "amor" must be Juan Carlos Vega.

Colombian Corn and Cheese Arepas

3 cups (about 1 pound) precooked white corn flour, like harina P.A.N.

2 tablespoons sugar

5 tablespoons unsalted butter, melted

1½ pounds soft fresh cheese like queso blanco or queso fresco (or mozzarella) coarsely grated (about 4 cups, well packed)

8 ounces aged cow's-milk cheese, preferably Mexican cotija (or Manchego or Parmesan), coarsely grated (about 2 cups)

1½ teaspoons salt

Mix flour and sugar in a bowl.

Add 3 cups warm water slowly. Mix with fingers. Add 4 tablespoons butter and then knead until it forms a soft dough.

Add the cheese one cup at a time and knead it into the dough. If the dough seems dry, add 1 to 2 tablespoons more water.

Taste the dough. Then if it requires salt, knead the salt in ½ teaspoon at a time. Knead the dough until it is soft and smooth and not lumpy. Cover the dough with a damp cloth and let it rest for 15 minutes.

Heat the broiler or grill over high heat.

Pull the dough into 11 sections of about ½ cup each (about 5 ounces). Roll each section into a ball, put on a tray, and cover with a slightly damp kitchen towel.

Then flatten the balls into thick circles, about 3½ inches in diameter. They should be flat on both sides. Return to tray and keep covered.

Line a broiler or grill rack with aluminum foil. Brush the foil with 1 tablespoon butter. Place arepas on the foil and broil or grill 4 inches from the heat source. Turn them once and cook until both sides are golden brown and speckled. This will take about 10 minutes per side.

Serve hot.

Adapted by permission of Julia Moskin at http://cooking.nytimes. com/recipes/1015180-colombian-corn-and-cheese-arepas.

Chapter 12

Summerton, a town of six thousand, where men still wore cowboy hats and the population was almost half Latino, had the feel of a slowly gentrifying frontier. Trendy wine bars, artisanal cheese stores, boutiques, and a fancy steakhouse mixed with tiny stores, their windows covered in posters of voluptuous women, where workers could buy their liquor in some privacy. It was so small that everyone knew each other's business, and Donna DeLacey, variously editor, reporter, and photographer with the *Summerton Post* for twenty years, knew most.

I'd met Donna at a wine festival in Summerton, and we'd hit it off. She was tart-tongued but also warm and open to adventure, so after my meeting with Teresa, I'd felt no hesitation e-mailing her out of the blue to ask if she'd be in her office the next day at 1:00 p.m. She'd e-mailed back where else *could* she be on a Thursday afternoon given the paper's schedule? If anyone would know about Collin Morehead, it was she, and since Summerton lay only fifteen miles from Arbor State, I would have plenty of time to get back for a meeting at 3:00 p.m. with Isobel, who'd e-mailed me early that morning to say that Yvonne had more to tell.

The office of the *Post* was located on the town's main street, but I would have missed it altogether if it were not for a small weather-beaten sign above the unprepossessing door. The large front office was crowded with empty desks, their tops strewn

163

with papers and computers. The walls were a crazy quilt of posters, awards, and more sheets of paper, along with a framed collection of political buttons. I could see Donna's back as she sat at her desk in a room that proved to be the size of a large closet. The wall behind her held shelves of bound volumes, which evidently contained past issues of the *Post*. The wall above her desk displayed a maze of cards, posters, pictures, and papers with curling edges. Open shelves to her left overflowed with random collections of boxes, tins, cups, aerosol cans, flashlights, and coils of black electronic cable. Things had settled in this office like mummified leavings, like detritus from the countless stories that had been filtered through the space.

"Donna?" I said. Donna looked up and stood to greet me. She was dressed in black and wore an enormous witch's hat. "You're kind of early for Halloween."

"I feel witchy today, so I've dressed the part." She was a robust, attractive woman with bleached blonde hair and a determined look. "Why have you come to Summerton on a Thursday afternoon?"

"I'm looking for information."

Donna tilted her face. She had a very sharp chin.

"Fire away. I get asked about stuff all the time."

"Do you know someone named Collin Morehead?"

"Oh yeah. He's a member of the City Council, and that's been my beat for years. He's one of those Arbor State types who come in with pie charts and graphs to argue about building an animal shelter. Folks around here don't relate to pie charts. They're more likely to say 'Well, I like dogs.' Want to get something to drink?"

"Sure."

Donna removed her hat and sailed it onto the papers covering her desk. "I used to sit in those endless meetings and think about all the ways someone could commit suicide using the stuff at hand."

"Hanging from the ceiling fan?"

"Yeah. And poking an artery with a sharp pen."

As we left the office, I caught a glimpse of printing presses in the next room.

"Is this where you print?"

"Naw, they're too old. Someone printed on them once."

I looked in. The presses were ancient and covered with dust.

"It's kind of a museum," Donna said. "But we haven't done much with it."

We walked to the wine bar a few doors down, an open, airy place with miles of shiny wooden floor, a case devoted to gourmet cheeses, a long bar with wines displayed on a full wall of racks, and small mosaic-topped tables and chairs. Places like this were part of Summerton's gentrification, but the wooden posts and rafters evoked a more rural history. At a table near a window, perfect for watching characters, suspicious or otherwise, we ordered two glasses of wine.

"Why not?" Donna said. "It's cocktail hour somewhere." She leaned back in her chair.

"So, Collin. I always thought it odd that he lives here. He strikes me as a corporate type, uptight, ambitious, not much interested in ordinary people. Most folks in this town are simple people—or want to appear simple." She paused to observe a man walk by the window wearing cowboy boots. "Some Arbor State professors live here to get away from the competitive atmosphere of the university. They coach soccer teams or sit on the council, and their Arbor State connections kind of disappear. But Morehead has never managed to fit in. The top button on his shirt was always buttoned, if you know what I mean, and he's a loner, divorced, and has a child living somewhere else, maybe Australia where he's from."

A cheerful young server delivered our glasses.

"I also know he's supported a number of corporate proposals to build housing developments on the fields. The proposals didn't go through, though. Most folks here don't want that kind of thing. And there've been rumors about his being involved in some kind of scandal Down Under." Donna raised her glass and I clinked mine.

"Scandal?" I took a sip of my wine, fruity without too much mineral in it, just how I liked it.

"Scandal . . . involving death . . . or possibly only wounding? Damn! I forget everything these days. He has a bad temper, evidently." Donna raised her own glass, swirled the wine, and gave it an investigative sniff.

"Do you think he'd be the type to poison a rival?"

"Who knows what lies in the human heart? There's a lot of darkness." Donna took a sip of wine, rolling it in her mouth. "Wait, are you trying to connect him to the poisoning at Arbor State?"

The small town news circuit knew all about the poisoning.

"I'm trying to track down leads. I'm a suspect in the case and so are some of my colleagues."

"Was it your corn bread, for God's sake?" Donna choked on her zinfandel. She and I had discussed my cooking in the past, and the police had finally released the detail about corn bread to the papers.

"Yes. You can imagine how I feel." I filled her in on the details of the case.

"I don't like the part about the phone calls, even though, God knows, I get plenty of loony letters and e-mails about my columns."

"On the advice of the police, I've asked the phone company to direct late night calls to a religious hotline."

"Oh damn, that's good. I wish I could do that with some of the trolls who write me. Prayer as punishment. I like it." Donna grinned, showing both of her dimples.

"I don't envy your job."

"You get used to it."

I said I was sure I'd never get used to it. We chatted for a while and then I said I had to go. My trip to Summerton had produced some interesting information about Collin's character, information that confirmed his interest in corporate profits and further suggested he had a violent streak. But I would have to process all that later. I had to see Isobel.

When we rose from the table, Donna gave me an assessing look.

"You don't look so good. You could use some goddess power. There's a celebration of Samhain up in the hills next Sunday. Some pagan women are getting together to mark the annual thinning of the veil between the world of spirits and our own."

"Maybe I do need goddess power, but I don't think I can make it to the hills." Someday, I'd have to attend one of these events just to find out what went on.

"I'll hold good thoughts for you."

★ ★ ★

A little before 3:00 p.m., I climbed the stairs of Haven Hall, the light from the bright autumn sky pouring into the stairwell like a sign from the heavens, and walked down the third-floor hallway on which Native American Studies had their offices. I stopped at the main office, which was painted in pale turquoise and lavender with posters of Indian baskets on the wall. Someone had tacked up a reminder: "Our lives are bound the way baskets are bound together." After exchanging greetings with the staff, I walked to Isobel's office and knocked on her door. Isobel opened, her earrings glinting silver through her hair. Yvonne sat in a chair next to Isobel's desk, her plump hands clasped tightly together. She looked tired, her mouth turned down at the corners.

The office wall behind Isobel had been recently decorated with a large abstract poster, half red, half yellow with native designs in blue and turquoise. Isobel, with her waterfall of dark hair, looked especially powerful against that backdrop. Isobel had often spoken about her grandmother, mother, and aunties, how they'd told her stories about standing tall and connecting with the energy of the earth. Stories, she said, were a form of power that made the past live again in the present. A line she'd recited from a Joy Harjo poem had stayed with me:

> "'Remember your birth, how your mother struggled
> to give you form and breath. You are evidence of
> her life, and her mother's, and hers.'"

I was ambivalent about my own mother's power, but I hoped that Isobel's would enliven Yvonne, whose face looked wan.

"Yvonne," Isobel said, "please tell us what you wanted to say."

"I know I'm going to get into trouble for this, but I have to tell someone. I saw and heard something before school started this fall that's been on my mind. I didn't want to share it with anyone else because it's private and Professor Elliott would have been incredibly angry if I had. It would have been the end of my job."

I nodded encouragingly, and then remembered Collin Morehead's ominous words during the meeting in the Office of Research: "We can also propose a cut in staff."

"My office is next to Professor Elliott's, and the office walls are thin. Sounds travel." Yvonne smoothed the edge of her gray jacket over its matching skirt. "I'd been to the ladies' room and was just returning when I saw Vice Provost Vogle go into Professor Elliott's office and shut the door. I went into my office to finish some work, and I heard them arguing. Dr. Vogle was very upset. I could hear her voice clearly, though not Professor Elliott's. He must have been trying to calm her down." Yvonne paused, her eyes wide. "And then I heard her shout, 'You said you loved me!' Professor Elliott said, 'Lower your voice, for God's sake.' I was so upset that I returned to the ladies' room until I thought it might be safe. I didn't want Professor Elliott to know what I'd heard or he'd never have trusted me again." Yvonne grasped her hands more tightly. "When I came back, he was shutting his office and leaving. I guess Dr. Vogle must have left too. I was so relieved because I thought he'd think I'd been out of the office for a while."

I listened in astonishment. Lorna and Peter? They seemed to move in two entirely different spheres. She was administration, and he was faculty, not that the two never mixed, but what had brought them together as lovers?

"I'm glad you told us, Yvonne," I said. "It was courageous of you, and I can't tell you how important this is."

"We'll do whatever we can," Isobel said, "to make sure you don't get into trouble." There was more than a bit of the woman warrior about Isobel.

Yvonne, eyes reddened, took her purse from the floor and opened it to get a tissue. She dotted her eyes and gently blew her nose.

"I should get back," Yvonne said. "I'm on my lunch hour, and the work is piling up." She left, quietly closing the door. Isobel and I looked at each other.

"Are you thinking what I'm thinking?" Isobel asked.

"Yes, but how did this come about? Did Lorna use my corn bread or did she bake her own? And why did she choose corn bread with goat cheese and caramelized onions?" Isobel shook her head as if to say the world held many mysteries.

★ ★ ★

I turned on my computer, began an Internet search for Lorna Vogle, found a copy of her curriculum vitae, and looked at her record of employment. She'd begun her career at Iowa State in

Wildlife and Ecology. She'd studied birds, specifically migratory birds. How odd, I thought. Lorna had never struck me as someone much interested in ecology or community, yet she'd studied creatures that depended on each other to escape hard weather and to find new sources of food. Had Lorna been more communal in her thinking back then?

Next, she'd been a dean at Cornell and had moved up the administrative ladder. Then Arbor State University and vice provost. What had converted her from studying wild birds to wearing jaunty suits and acting like a corporate officer? I began searching references to Peter Elliott. "Oh, for heaven's sake," I said out loud. He too had been at Iowa State in Plant Pathology. But he'd stayed on after Lorna left for Cornell and then had taken a job at Arbor State five years before she'd arrived. Had they known each other at Iowa? I wondered. And, if so, in what capacity? Had Lorna thought he'd loved her then too?

I entered the words "Furadan" and "migratory birds." A page full of articles popped up. Before it had been banned in the early 1990s, granular Furadan had killed a million migratory birds each year. And liquid Furadan was still in use. Sometimes 92 percent of a flock would die after landing on a field treated with liquid Furadan. "Birds killed by Furadan," I typed in. The list included blue birds, robins, and red-winged blackbirds. I settled in and stopped only when my desk was overflowing with downloaded articles on Furadan, migratory birds, and bird poisonings in Iowa cornfields. That Lorna was familiar with Furadan seemed obvious, but how was she connected to my corn bread? I knew whom to ask.

I stepped across the hall and knocked on my young colleague Callie's door.

"Emily! Come in."

"Do you have a minute?"

"Sure. Have a seat."

Callie had erected a screen in her office, and entering was a bit like going through a labyrinth. One side of the screen was adorned with a poster of African masks. On the other side, an African cloth of black, white, and brown covered a narrow cot. One wall was painted an earthy red.

"I'm trying to figure something out. Please don't tell anyone what I'm about to share because if I'm wrong I'd be in trouble. I have reason to think that Lorna poisoned Peter."

"You're kidding." Her large eyes widened.

"I've learned they had a relationship. I think she was angry because he was trying to break it off, but I can't figure out how she could have managed the poisoning. She wasn't at the Native American reception, and what evidence is there that she would make corn bread with goat cheese and caramelized onions?"

"Oh, Em." Callie looked stricken. "You served that corn bread last spring at the Women's Studies reception, remember? And I asked you for the recipe and you e-mailed it to me? Lorna dropped by that event."

"I remember seeing her briefly. She wasn't there long. I was surprised she came at all, given her lack of interest in the program."

"She was there long enough to eat a piece of corn bread. We were standing at the table and she asked me who'd made it and I told her you, and she'd said she'd love to have the recipe. I told her that I'd ask you for it and e-mail her a copy, which I must have done. If so, she could have put poison in her own batch."

"Furadan kills migratory birds. Perhaps she saw Peter as someone who'd poisoned her life. Do you still have that e-mail?"

Callie scrolled through her lists.

"Let's see." She typed Lorna Vogle into the search engine under recipients.

"Yes, I do. There's an advantage to never cleaning out your files. Here, I'll print it out."

I took Callie's printout and stepped back to my office to call Lorna's secretary.

"I'd like an appointment with the vice provost," I said to the staff person, a woman with whom I was friendly. "It won't take long. Does she have anything available?"

"She's had a cancellation. Ordinarily, I'd just leave the time open, but since it's you, Dr. Addams—you're always so cordial with the staff—I could squeeze you in for thirty minutes tomorrow morning at eleven. What shall I say this is about?"

"You can say it's about the Haven Hall programs and our proposal to become a separate division. Thanks so much." What if I were wrong about this? My mouth felt dry. I'd have to think about my approach carefully.

An e-mail from Alma appeared on my screen.

"Emily, we're having a Dia de los Muertos party on Monday, November 1 at 4:00 p.m. Please come and bring something to share."

"I'd love to," I wrote. Well, it won't be corn bread this time, I thought.

★ ★ ★

At home that evening Polly and I made candy corn cupcakes for the upcoming Halloween party in Polly's class. I was glad to have this pleasurable escape. The cupcakes were made from a white cake batter, one half of which was tinted with orange food coloring and the other half with yellow. The idea was to layer the two colors in the cupcake pans, bake and frost them with white frosting, and then decorate them with candy corn. It was the kind of involved project that Polly loved. Like her mother, she had a passion for celebrating holidays with ritual foods.

Sadie sat on her red-gold haunches at the end of the kitchen counter, looking hopeful.

"No, Sadie, this isn't good for you," Polly said.

Sadie was a sweet dog, but I had been unsuccessful so far in training her not to steal food. The month before, I'd made a dozen lemon cupcakes for Polly's class. I'd gone out of the kitchen for a few minutes, and when I'd returned, the cupcakes had disappeared. For a moment I thought I'd lost my mind. What've I done with the cupcakes? I'd asked myself. It had taken several minutes to realize that Sadie had scarfed down every one. Later that week the yard had been full of Sadie's poop with pieces of paper cupcake holder mixed in.

"Sadie, we can go for a walk," Polly said soothingly. Sadie thumped her heavy golden tail upon the floor. She understood the word "walk."

Halloween, for reasons I couldn't fathom, was Polly's favorite holiday, even surpassing Christmas. There was something about the weather at Halloween—the increasing crispness of the air, the rustling of dead leaves on sycamore trees—that stirred Polly. She seemed to have inherited a special sensitivity to the idea of spirits as well. Where did that come from? At times I, myself, felt that Miriam's spirit was with me. Why were Polly and I so easily moved by the idea of the unseen? Had it come from the tiny bit of Shoshone in my father's family line? Since the relationship in question had not involved marriage and had involved a person who wasn't white, that part of our heritage had been a family secret. My father had only divulged that history near the end of his life.

"What do you want to be for Halloween this year?" I asked.

"The Bride of Frankenstein."

I sighed.

"Don't you want to be something more cheerful?"

Three years ago Polly had dressed up as the Little Mermaid, but after that it had been a black cat and then a witch. Where was this progression going to end? Polly, with her mass of brown curls and azure eyes, looked more like a princess than a monster bride.

"I like to be scary. It makes me feel strong."

I sighed again. Outwardly Polly had taken her parents' divorce very well, maybe too well. I knew that the break had hurt my daughter deeply. Perhaps death-related costumes were a way of revisiting, and then controlling, the pain. Were they Polly's way of expressing what, ordinarily, she kept to herself? My chest ached as I looked at the spray of freckles on Polly's well-loved face.

"Okay, the Bride of Frankenstein it is. Your dad has you this Sunday, which is Halloween, so you'll do the neighborhood trick-or-treating with him. But the downtown trick-or-treating is on Saturday, so we'll do that together." Halloween was a lot more fun when Polly was with me, and now, especially, I looked forward to her cheerful presence. I was sure to need it after my visit to Lorna Vogle.

—

Candy Corn
Halloween Cupcakes

Vanilla Cupcakes

1¾ cups all-purpose flour

1½ teaspoons baking powder

½ teaspoon baking soda

½ teaspoon salt

¼ cup unsalted butter, softened

1 cup granulated sugar

2 large eggs

¼ cup soybean oil or vegetable oil

⅓ cup sour cream

1 tablespoon vanilla extract

⅔ cup milk (whole, 2%, skim—any kind will work)

Yellow and red food coloring

Candy corn for decorating★

Vanilla Frosting

3½ tablespoons heavy whipping cream

2½ cups powdered sugar

6 tablespoons butter, softened

2 teaspoons vanilla extract

Cupcakes

Preheat the oven to 350°F

Line cupcake pan with paper liners.

In a medium-sized mixing bowl, combine flour, baking powder, baking soda, and salt. Mix together.

In another bowl, cream sugar and butter together with an electric mixer until light and fluffy.

Add the creamed butter and sugar to the flour mixture and mix on medium-low speed for about a minute. You will end up with a crumb texture.

Add eggs, oil, sour cream, and vanilla to the flour mixture and beat on medium speed until just combined. Slowly add the milk on low speed.

Evenly divide the batter into 2 bowls. Add yellow food coloring to one bowl. For the second bowl add yellow and red food coloring to make orange. (The ratio for creating orange is 2 drops of yellow for each drop of red).

Fill cupcake liners ¼ full with the yellow batter, then fill to about ½ full with orange batter.

Bake for 14–16 minutes (if you are making mini cupcakes, bake for 12–14 minutes) until an inserted toothpick comes out clean. Or gently tap the top of the cupcake with your finger. If it springs back, it's done.

Remove from the oven and let cool in the pan for a few minutes, then move to a wire rack to finish cooling.

Frosting

Combine ingredients and beat on medium speed with mixer until you have the consistency you want.

Add a little extra whipping cream if you want the frosting thinner or add more powdered sugar to thicken it. If you're going to pipe the frosting, you want it fairly thick.

*Wait to place the candy corn on top of the cupcakes until you are about ready to serve them or store cupcakes in the refrigerator to prevent the candy corn from melting onto the frosting (trust me, if you leave them at room temperature overnight, the candy corn melts and the colors run onto the frosting).

Adapted by permission of Holly and Katie at The SemiSweet Sisters http://www.thesemisweetsisters.com/2014/09/19/ candy-corn-halloween-cupcakes/.

Chapter 13

The rain came, a real rain at last. The wet winter for which Arborville was famous might finally have arrived. As I folded my umbrella and pushed through the doors of Murk Hall, my stomach tightened, as if I were going with a cup in my hand on behalf of Women's Studies. But, for the first time, I wasn't going to Lorna's office to plead for something on behalf of the program. The purpose of my visit was far more risky and unsettling. What if I'd gotten it wrong? What if Lorna produced some story that sent my own intuited narrative crashing to the ground? I wondered what the consequence would be for that kind of insubordination. Maybe I could have gone to the police first, but there wasn't enough evidence for that. And, at any rate, my visits with potential suspects and my hours of gleaning information had made me determined to understand things for myself. At this point, I needed to see Lorna. I had to know.

I thought briefly of Donna in her witch's hat, of Isobel looking larger than life in front of the red poster, of Polly feeling powerful when she dressed as something frightening. Perhaps,, I thought, I'll just make myself look big and scary, the way you're supposed to do when facing off with a mountain lion. I rode the elevator to the main administrative office, a warren of carpeted dividers, and made my way to Lorna's office. I greeted Lorna's secretary, an older woman with a halo of white hair.

"Professor Addams. Let me give the vice provost a buzz. Professor Addams is here," she said into the phone.

Lorna opened the door. Her office was not large but it held a heavy wooden desk and a round table with four upholstered chairs in a dull teal. There was nothing to make the space seem homey, no pictures on the desk, not even a plant to break up the dreariness.

"Have a seat." Lorna indicated the table. I took a chair and Lorna sat opposite, wearing a black suit with one of her ever-present scarves—this one black and red with a tinge of yellow. Black and red with a tinge of yellow? The combination seemed familiar. And then I recalled the red-winged blackbird I had seen on my walk with Wilmer, and for the first time it struck me that Lorna often dressed herself in the colors of migratory birds. Did she miss her former life? Was there a conflict in her that I had never recognized? Maybe I had failed to see the deeper meaning of her costumes.

"What can I do for you?" Lorna asked brightly.

"I know about the corn bread." I was looking directly into Lorna's eyes. I hadn't planned to begin so abruptly, but the words blew out.

"What are you talking about?"

I watched as Lorna pulled the scarf slightly away from her neck. So it's true, I thought. You did make the corn bread. I felt the anger stirring in my body.

"I think you were the one who told the police to ask me about my corn bread."

"I have no idea what you mean."

"Someone told me about the argument you had with Peter. This person heard you shout, 'You said you loved me.'" Words were gusting from me like part of a gathering storm. "I know you had a relationship with him and I know that Callie gave you the recipe for my corn bread last spring."

"This is nonsense." Lorna spoke with less conviction than before. She had grown unusually still in her chair.

"You were angry about his relationships with Mei Lee and maybe Jenny Archer as well. And you must have known about the double dipping." Bits of information swirled now like household furniture being shed by a tornado. "I found out about that too." Lorna placed a hand on her scarf once more and then set it back, with some deliberation, on the table.

"This is absurd. Where are you getting this information?" A reddish pink, the color of a rose finch, crept into Lorna's cheek.

"Women talk to each other on this campus." Staff might seem invisible to those in power, but they had eyes and ears and consciences. It was because women did talk to each other that I'd found out about Lorna and Peter. "Callie still has the e-mail in which she sent you my recipe."

"That proves nothing," Lorna said, but made no movement to show me the door.

She can't throw me out, I reasoned, because she knows it's true and she wants to prevent me from telling anyone else. Still, confronting Lorna with a jumble of evidence had not gotten me very far, and, on an impulse, I tried a different approach.

"You and Peter began at Iowa State, isn't that true?" I said it in a gentle way, as if Lorna and I were friends or confidantes. "And then you became involved with him. That's something I can understand. You must have been lonely. Many single people are. I know I sometimes am, and you were a woman in science. I understand that can be isolating."

I watched as Lorna's face trembled and her body almost imperceptibly began to droop.

"How did you connect?" I asked in a kindly way. "Was it on campus? Did your work bring you together somehow?" Lorna sat silent for a long moment. I inclined my head in what I hoped was an encouraging way. "Was it off campus, then?"

Another silence, this one longer as Lorna's body slumped back against her chair.

"In a café in downtown Ames," Lorna said, at last, as if talking to herself. "If I had walked my usual route, it might never have happened. I'd never have met him in that intimate way, might never have gotten involved."

"But it didn't work out."

"He was married. He's always married, but it never means a thing to him. Peter is a hungry man."

"And you left Iowa because of him." I was guessing, filling in a story that seemed way too familiar. I remembered that Lorna's parents had died young and that she'd been raised by a distant, old-fashioned aunt. Maybe that was why romantic love had played such a dramatic role in her life. I understood the need for love and family—all too well.

"Yes, I took a different path. I became dean at Cornell and moved up the ladder. The top administration there were interested in seeing women advance—as long as the women did what they were told."

"And you came to Arbor State because Peter was here," I continued.

"That wasn't the only reason." Lorna pressed her shoulders back into her chair. "It's a good job. I thought I could move up."

Did Lorna imagine that she could become chancellor? Women who'd been on campus for any length of time knew that such a move was highly unlikely. If women had been around for a while, they knew too much, harbored resentments, and men in power sensed that and were wary.

"And you became involved with him again," I prompted, "and then you found out about Mei Lee and maybe others."

"Peter was such a pig," Lorna spat out.

An insult to pigs, although pigs did fight each other for dominance, biting each other's ears and tails until a hierarchy was established. But oughtn't one to expect more from one's human companions?

"What about the double dipping? You must have known about that, too." Lorna gave the door a quick glance.

"When I found out about Mei Lee, I threatened to go to the Conflict of Interest Committee and to the Office of Research, but Peter said he would meet with the committee himself and tell them that I knew about the double dipping and didn't report it. Peter could be vindictive if he was crossed. And in the end, the heaviest penalty would have fallen on me. It would have cost me my job. He was going to take that away from me too."

Along with your heart, I thought.

"You knew who disagreed with him on campus because he told you. You knew about the panel because he told you about that, too, and you threw suspicion on other people by feeding the police anonymous tips. You were the one who suggested I was known for making corn bread with goat cheese and caramelized onions."

Lorna looked into the blank sky outside the office window. The rain had stopped.

"I was only trying to buy time to think. I didn't mean to hurt anyone. And, in the end, I didn't even mean to hurt Peter."

"But you gave him the corn bread."

Lorna breathed deeply, now openly tugging at her scarf.

"I'd asked him to come to my house for a drink."

I pictured them in the grand hall of that sprawling home in Palomino Hills. I'd noticed the house seemed formal. Maybe Lorna had tried to make it homier by expanding her cooking repertoire. As everyone knew, one sure way to Peter's heart was through food.

"I made the corn bread, but I only used enough Furadan to make him sick so he'd miss the meeting with the committee while I thought about what to do. As vice provost, I'm responsible for reporting financial irregularities." Lorna's eyes looked glazed as though she were getting sick. "But, in the end, I couldn't offer him the corn bread. I left it on the counter in the kitchen. Peter wouldn't listen to me. He threatened me, told me to leave him alone. I was so upset, I ran upstairs and locked myself in my bedroom. The next morning I saw that some of the bread was missing. Peter must have helped himself on his way out. That was Peter, always eating, always sticking his fingers into things, carrying food around in his pockets."

I had a vision of Peter standing pink-faced in the corridor by one of the pens stuffing his paunchy self with pieces of corn bread, waiting for his estranged young mistress to feed his animals.

"Peter deserved what he got," Lorna said. "He was toxic, like Furadan entering the ecosystem."

I looked at Lorna in her black suit. Her scarf was awry. Tears had reddened her eyes. She seemed vulnerable, a wild bird, trapped. I felt sorry for her. Love, and then revenge, had trumped ambition. It was a familiar story, an age-old melo-drama, a woman's romance.

"Did you ever follow Peter or send him e-mails?"

"Never. And why would I follow him? What would be the point of that?"

"None, I guess. You know I'll have to tell the police every-thing I've heard."

Lorna looked as if she were facing a long migration. "Yes," she said and that was all.

★ ★ ★

Pools of rain glimmered on streets and sidewalks as I walked from the administration building to the police station on the opposite side of campus. Best to tell this story in person, I thought, hoping that Sergeants Dorothy Brown or Gina Garcia would be there. As I walked through campus, a flock of geese passed over me, in their eternal V formation, honking noisily, necks extended before them, on their annual journey. The air was chilly in the late afternoon, and I shivered.

I entered the low, squat, cinder block police station, went up to the window, and asked for Sergeant Brown. In a few moments she stepped through a side door.

"Professor Addams, come on back." Sergeant Brown led me to a small room furnished with a metal table and some chairs.

"Would you like some coffee?"

I said I was fine.

"I've been to see Lorna Vogle, and I need to tell you what I found out." I felt no pleasure in what I began to relate.

"What a story," Dorothy said when I'd finished. "It's almost like a romance novel."

"Yes, only there's no happy ending for Lorna."

"We'll check it out. In the meantime, there are two pieces of good news I can share. Professor Elliott's come out of his coma. The doctors think he's going to pull through."

I felt a rush of relief. Lorna wouldn't be tried for murder. And then I realized I'd come full circle with her, this woman who'd secretly, and not so secretly, worked against the well-being, indeed the existence, of the Haven Hall programs. I puzzled for a moment over this transformation in my feelings. Strictly speaking, Lorna had tried to silence Peter to save her own job, but her collusion with Peter had come from sources more deeply rooted and, in their way, more tenderhearted. They'd come from longing, from a need for love, from the thrill of desiring a very wrong man. I was familiar with those feelings from my early days with Solomon. I looked around the bare office. Like me, Lorna had had passions and painful losses too, and though that hardly let her off the hook for having wanted to make Peter sick and for having threatened our community, they proved she'd had a heart.

"Also," Dorothy continued, leaning over the metal table,

"we've traced some of the suspects in the vandalism case. It seems that the cornfields they destroyed had been sprayed with pesticides. Some members of Save the Fields must have gotten contaminated because there were three visits to the local emergency room about four hours after the attacks. Three young people came in with dizziness, vomiting, and blurred vision. We tracked them down and have picked them up." Dorothy folded her strong-looking hands neatly before her.

"Did one of them drive a dark blue van?"

"How did you know that?" Dorothy cocked her head to the side.

"Tess Ryan thought she was being followed by such a vehicle. It was a guess."

Now, maybe I did know what a member of Save the Fields looked like. I remembered my fierce, red-haired kickboxing colleague. They looked like everyone else.

★ ★ ★

Wilmer and I sat in the Café Giorgio, a smart, casual restaurant where customers ordered their meals from the chalkboard and carried their wine to the table. I chose my favorite meal— mixed greens with goat cheese and almonds and grilled salmon with brown butter and almond sauce. Even in Arborville's downtown, you could eat very well. Wilmer and I settled into a table next to the open kitchen where we could feel the warmth from the pizza ovens and the grill. The aromas of roasting fish and melting cheese were concentrated in this corner, and I liked the coziness of the padded, rust-colored banquette. I settled into it and took a sip of sauvignon blanc.

"So you see," I said, "meeting Peter at that café changed her whole life. There she was studying migratory birds, thinking about ecological systems and biodiversity, giving value to the smallest kinds of life, and the next minute she was off to Cornell for a career in administration, which brought her to

Arbor State where she's been living the life of a corporate officer, maximizing profit and trying to get rid of what her bosses
seem to see as unproductive units in a giant factory." I paused
for a moment to take a bite of the buttery salmon. "If she hadn't
walked down that street in Ames, Iowa, with the café on it, she
might never have met Peter in a personal way. I wonder what
her life would have been like."

"It's an interesting coincidence," Wilmer said.

"Oh, is it like the Butterfly Effect? Does a chance meeting in Iowa set off a tornado in California?" I was thinking of
my blustery encounter with Lorna. "Does a small change at
one place precipitate a nonlinear result in another? I kind of
understand it now." I looked at Wilmer, who would undoubt-
edly have liked to revise my account of the Butterfly Effect, but
instead gave me a broad country smile. I felt a sudden urge to
kiss him. He looked back at me fondly.

"You're changing me," he said.

"How?"

"Before I met you I'd never given a thought to inequalities
on campus. Now I can't stop seeing them. Now it matters."

I beamed at Wilmer and laid my hand on his from across
the table.

"I'm learning from you too." That's what a relationship
could do. It could draw you into another person's world, into
another's perspective. It could enlarge your mind and also
your emotions. I studied Wilmer's friendly face. Was there a
future with him? He was smart, and intuitive as well, and I was
beginning to see his humorous side. And now he had begun to
take an interest in the causes about which I was so passionate.
Only time would tell. I knew from my painful experience with
Solomon that relationships, no matter how pleasing to begin
with, didn't always pan out.

"There's one thing I don't understand," I said at last. "Three
women—Mei Lee, Jenny, and Teresa—mentioned that Peter

had undergone a change in the last few months. Teresa said he'd gotten distant, more secretive about his work, and imagined at times he was being followed. I don't know what to make of it. Lorna hadn't been following him, and there'd be no reason for Mei Lee or Jenny to have done so."

"It's his research," Wilmer said, as decisively as if he'd solved a math problem with black ink on white paper. "He might have gotten results that someone else was very interested in."

"That didn't occur to me." I couldn't imagine anyone being overly invested in finding out about my essay on shrimp and grits. So things weren't settled after all. There was more to the Peter Elliott case than I'd discovered.

★ ★ ★

The next day, Polly and I walked the streets of downtown Arborville, the sidewalks clogged with fairies, action figures, belly dancers, wizards, princesses, and cats. Polly was wearing her Bride of Frankenstein ensemble—a long black wig, white face, black mouth, and a long white gown we'd found in a secondhand store and which I'd shortened. It was a striking contrast. Ghoulishness in broad daylight on the prosaic sidewalks of a small town that prided itself on its down-home atmosphere.

What was Halloween anyway? Even now, as I knew from Donna, some people believed the veil between the living and the spirit world grew thin as harvest approached, signaling a time of winter and the dying of leaves, the migration of birds, and the diminishment of the sun. For centuries, Halloween had been a time of placating harmful spirits who might have represented early people's fears that the sun and growth and living things would never return. To ward off the darkness, people had taken embers from a common bonfire and placed them in lanterns made of carved turnips, precursors of the jack-o'-lantern.

I looked into the gutter where brown leaves had been swept

into piles. Halloween marked the end of harvest and served as a time of contemplating one's own mortality and of ritually managing the dread associated with death. Community rituals asserted the continuation of life and the power of the community over the forces of darkness and despair. They helped assuage the haunting fear of mortality and were therefore vital to human life. I thought of Isobel before the fire, how the flames had seemed to draw us all together. It being late October now, I felt a chill.

Everyone, it occurred to me, is haunted by something. Isobel was haunted by her nephew's death, Alma, by her parents' lives, and I, by the loneliness of my childhood and by the death of Miriam, along with the comfort and beauty she'd once brought to the world. Polly and I both were haunted by the unraveling of our family and by the loss of a security we'd once shared. But loss, I'd learned, is sometimes necessary. My marriage to Solomon had made me angry, unhappy, insecure, and worse. It had produced a noxious environment for Polly. So Solomon and I had divorced, and Polly dressed up as a witch, a black cat, a Bride of Frankenstein, to keep the scary void at bay.

But where was Polly? I'd been so immersed in my reflections on Halloween that I hadn't noticed she was no longer at my side. Had she gone into a store without me? I looked up and down the streets and into the dress shop just behind. She was nowhere to be seen. The sidewalks grew more crowded, but I stood fixed to the spot, not wanting to leave, so Polly, if she'd just wandered off, could find me again. Two men in black suits passed by. How odd. No one wore suits in Arborville, much less black ones. Were they in costume? Or were they using Halloween to make their way along the streets without provoking comment? Were there other men like them on the streets today, perhaps looking for vulnerable children? What kind of mother was I not to notice Polly's absence? What if I didn't find her? I hurried into the boutique behind me.

"Have you seen a ten-year-old girl dressed like the Bride of Frankenstein?"

The owner of the store, who was wearing gothic black, looked puzzled.

"There are so many kids in and out. I haven't noticed."

I hurried back to my spot in the sidewalk and looked up and down the block. The streets seemed to hold fewer ballerinas now—more monsters, more skeletons, and more ghosts. I looked up the street. A crowd had gathered in the parking lot that divided the blocks of stores, as if people were gathered around a sight. Were they gathered around Polly? Had something happened to her? My chest constricted.

"Please," I said. "Please, let her be all right." Life without Polly stretched before me, empty, incomprehensible. I ran to the crowd and edged my way in. Parents and their costumed children were packed tight.

"Excuse me," I said. "Excuse me. I'm looking for my daughter." A woman dressed as a witch looked at me with sympathy and made room for me to move past her.

"What does she look like?" she asked. Her own daughter was holding her mother's hand.

"She's dressed like the Bride of Frankenstein in white."

The woman looked round the crowd.

"There?" she said, pointing.

And there Polly was, looking cheerful despite her white face and black mouth, watching a man dressed as a mime riding a unicycle. I made my way to her side, my chest emptied of blood.

"Polly! Why did you wander off like that without telling me?"

"Mom, I did tell you." She wrinkled her forehead at me. "Maybe you didn't hear me because you were thinking too hard."

I had been thinking too hard. It was a problem from which I sometimes suffered.

"You're right." I gathered Polly to me. "But, shake me out of it next time before you take off, okay?"

"I will. Don't worry, Mom."

I'd upset Polly too.

"It's okay. It's my fault. It's just . . . what would I do without you?" I'd had a brush with death, but now the blood surged in me again. Polly was safe, was at my side, still with me, and suddenly everything seemed within my reach. As a flock of small birds made its way across the pale sky, I felt I could do anything. Perhaps, I could even find out what I didn't yet know about the case of Peter Elliott.

Corn Bread with Caramelized Onions and Goat Cheese

1 cup coarse corn-meal (also packaged as "polenta") but regular cornmeal will also work

2 cups buttermilk

1 to 2 tablespoons oil, butter, or a combination thereof

2 cups onion in a ¾-inch dice

1¾ cups unbleached, all-purpose flour

1½ tablespoons baking powder

¼ teaspoon baking soda

1 teaspoon salt

6-ounce log of goat cheese, at room temperature

3 large eggs, at room temperature

2 tablespoons unsalted butter, melted

2 tablespoons honey

¼ cup granulated sugar

2½ cups fresh or frozen corn kernels

2 tablespoons bacon fat, vegetable oil, or butter

The night before baking the corn bread, soak the cornmeal in the buttermilk. Cover and leave at room temperature overnight. (Although this step is optional, you might appreciate it if you use coarse cornmeal or if you often find corn bread on the gritty side.) If you don't do this in advance, mix them before you start the next step.

Preheat the oven to 350°F.

Heat a large sauté pan to medium and coat the bottom with 1 to 2 tablespoons of oil, butter, or a combination thereof. Add the onions and cook them until they're well caramelized with browned edges. Season with salt and set aside.

Sift together the flour, baking powder, baking soda, and salt and set aside.

In a large mixing bowl, beat the goat cheese until fluffy.

Add the eggs one at a time and scrape down the bowl between each. (It may look a little curdled at this point, but don't worry. It all comes back together in the oven.)

Add the melted butter, honey, sugar, and cornmeal/buttermilk mixture and mix until smooth. Add the flour mixture and stir until combined and then gently stir in the corn kernels, mixing them until the ingredients are evenly distributed.

Place two tablespoons of bacon fat, vegetable oil, or butter in a 10-inch round cake pan (you can also use a cast-iron skillet, 9 by 13-inch baking pan, or a 12-inch square pan).

Place the pan in the oven for 5 to 7 minutes, until the fat gets very hot. With good pot holders, remove the pan and tilt it to grease the corners and sides.

Pour in the batter, spreading it evenly, and sprinkle the caramelized onion evenly over the top.

Bake for about 30 minutes, or until the corn bread is firm and springing (the baking time will depend on the size and type of pan) and a toothpick inserted into the center comes out clean.

Allow the bread to cool in the pan for at least 15 minutes before slicing it into squares or wedges.

Serve immediately.

Chapter 14

As I drove west on Paintbrush Boulevard the next morning, passing a bicycle path, bordered by a double row of olive trees, a single red-tailed hawk flapped twice, launching itself into air. The sight of a hawk's glide always brought me to life, making me feel as if I too were capable of soaring. On the other side of the trees, where Arborville became more rural and the university stretched into seemingly endless flat fields, I began to look carefully to the right for a craftsman bungalow with green trim, and when I found it, I turned into its long and dusty driveway. I was visiting Tess for a "cup of tea," which was her way of telling me that the visit would not be long. On the phone I'd told Tess only that I had important information about the poisoning, something I wanted to share in person. I hoped Tess, who had an insider's view of scientific protocols, could shed more light on what rules Lorna and Peter had actually broken.

I got out of the car to the sound of chickens erupting into clucks from somewhere in the back. Tess and her husband maintained a small organic farm, and I could see a barn and, just in front of it, a large garden. A pathway, lined with rosemary, lavender, and sage, led to a front porch where a scarecrow dressed in farmer's clothes was stuffed onto a swinging bench. A row of carved pumpkins lined one side of the doorway, displaying the outlines of a ghost, a frowning tree, and a startled owl. Tess answered my knock, alight with her usual energy.

"Thanks for letting me come. You've got a charming place here."

"We'll have some tea and I'll show you around. I made corn bread."

"Without Furadan, I hope."

"I swear. It's clean, and it's made of genetically engineered corn."

I must have looked surprised because Tess went on to explain.

"I make a practice of cooking with GMOs. It's my way of showing that I believe in my own and my colleagues' research and in the research of scientists the world over who've found that the GMOs on the market so far are safe."

Two tabby cats sauntered toward me and entwined themselves around my ankles.

"Hi, kitties," I said, scratching them both behind their ears. I sometimes wished that Sadie could abide a feline.

We went through the living and dining rooms, where toys belonging to Tess's children were tucked into various corners, and entered the kitchen, which was large with wide windows looking onto the garden. A wooden country table stood in the middle, with a vase of yellow and purple wildflowers at its center. Tess put a teakettle on the stove and gathered cups and boxes of herbal teas from an overstuffed kitchen cabinet. The place felt homey, felt like the house of a woman who had her feet on the ground.

After Tess poured tea and she and I were comfortably face-to-face, I gave her the details of my visit to Lorna Vogle. Tess's eyebrows rounded into her forehead as she listened.

"This is astonishing." Tess went on to explain the legalities of what Peter and Lorna had done. "Peter has broken absolutely every rule. Lorna knew and even though she's vice provost, she didn't tell anyone! She's in such terrible trouble."

"I think we should keep this quiet until the police decide

what to do with her." The idea of exposing Lorna's painful love story to everyone on campus seemed distasteful to me now. "Bad as it was to think of making Peter sick, Peter's deal with Syndicon is part of a much wider and more harmful pattern of behavior."

Tess nodded. "It's incredibly frustrating because GMO technology could do the world such good. It could address the problem of world hunger and, in fact, it already is. There's a rice being developed right now that is enriched with beta carotene. It could massively cut down the number of children dying from vitamin A deficiency around the world." Tess took a large sip of tea, as if clearing her throat. "My husband and I have been thinking about a way to combine genetic engineering with organic farming. Organic farming is about using fewer pesticides and synthetic fertilizers, but up to now that's meant losing a large percentage of the crop. To feed the world at the rate it's growing we'd need to double crop yields by 2050."

I liked hearing Tess talk. It made me feel hopeful about the future.

"The worst thing for the environment is farming." Tess leaned over the table. "It destroys the native ecosystem and uses fertilizers and irrigation. Fertilizer runoffs from large farms get into water tables and cause massive algae blooms in the oceans. But we have to farm because we have to eat." Tess's cheeks had turned their peony rose again. "And even with organic farming you have to degrade the fields with plows and tractors. Organic farms are labor-intensive and require large tracts of land. If it were to become widespread, it would destroy even more land and use even more water."

"Oh, the corn bread." Tess jumped up, brought a pan to the table, found some small plates, and cut us each a square. The corn bread, still warm and crumbly, tasted sweet and healthy.

"But if we could develop crops that were more efficient in

using nitrogen or water and that improved the health of the soil, we'd go a long way toward feeding the world."

"Is it that corporations like Syndicon have given genetic engineering as a whole a bad name?" I asked.

"When I ask most people about their objections, it comes down to that. I hate Syndicon. That's where their anger comes in. A lot of people object to the way corporations like Syndicon own seeds and technologies and use that for their own profits. Some of their seeds produce large yields, but we can't rely on corporations to help subsistence farmers. It's not in their self-interest. That's where foundations and publicly funded research come in. Seeds and technologies developed in the public domain can and are being freely shared with developing nations." The rose in Tess's cheeks deepened. "What matters is to create sustainable agricultures that can feed the world without damaging it."

Despite all the bad things I had heard about GMOs, I was inclined to believe Tess. Syndicon's did not need to be the only model of how new technologies could work.

"You give me hope," I said, taking another bite of the corn bread. I chewed it slowly, savoring its mild flavor. "There's something else I wanted to ask you about." I went on to tell Tess about Peter's uneasiness over the summer, before Save the Fields had left its mark.

"A friend of mine suggested that someone might be after Peter's data."

"It sounds possible. Peter was involved in a number of shady operations. Perhaps he tied himself, in some way, to shady characters as well. That can get you in a lot of trouble."

A high bleating sound from the yard interrupted the course of our conversation.

"That's our goat," Tess said. "Come, I'll show you around."

★ ★ ★

I slouched comfortably in my reading chair that afternoon with the completed essay on shrimp and grits. I was going to proof it one last time, but just as I picked up my favorite pencil—Ticonderoga 2½, not too hard, not too soft—the phone rang.

"Emily Addams?" a voice with a Spanish accent asked.

"Teresa?" I wasn't expecting a call from Peter's wife.

"Yes. Emily, the police just left my house. While I was at the hospital this afternoon, someone broke in and went through Peter's study. They took his computer and pried into a locked drawer."

"Were they looking for his research?"

"Peter didn't keep information about his research at home. It's in his office. I think I should go there. Whatever the issue is, I want to know about it first. I owe him that."

"I'll come with you. Do you have a key to Peter's office and the building?" It was Sunday, and many places on campus would be locked.

"Yes, he had an extra set made for me."

"I'll pick you up."

Fifteen minutes later I rang Teresa's doorbell, and Teresa answered, wearing a black sweater and black jeans just like me.

"We match," I said. "We look like we're dressed for Halloween."

"We need skeletons down our fronts. Tomorrow's El Dia de los Muertos."

I tried to imagine the two of us as the bony folk figures that marked the holiday. I envisioned a skeletal, but still lovely, Teresa dressed in a long fuchsia skirt with yellow roses in her hair. At the end of her life, Miriam had been skeletal as well, but she had retained her fragile beauty, had worn a Japanese bed jacket printed in rosy flowers, had pinned her hair into a fashionable knot on top of her head. Miriam had died on the first of November. When I thought of her, I felt my own life pressing against the kitchen knife of our shared mortality.

"Let's take my car," Teresa said. "I have a parking permit for Bauman Hall."

Teresa turned right off Wild Deer Lane and continued past the squat tan buildings of the elementary school that Polly had attended, finally crossing Paintbrush Boulevard, where Ceanothus separated the main campus from the roads to the airport and the fields.

"You're a neighbor and a colleague," Teresa said. "I didn't know who else to call."

"I'm glad you did. You shouldn't have to do this by yourself."

Teresa, I thought, must have been reluctant to call Juan Carlos, with whom she was most certainly involved, lest she run into any of Peter's colleagues while getting to his office.

"How's Peter?"

"He's out of the coma and the doctors think he'll be talking soon." Teresa paused, bit her lip, and looked at her long hands on the steering wheel. On her left hand was a slender golden wedding ring and on another a small gold band set with an emerald. I'd read somewhere that emeralds were plentiful in Colombia.

"There's something funny going on. I've been seeing a pair of men in black suits lounging around the front entrance to the hospital or sometimes sitting in a car parked close to the lobby. I didn't make much of it until today when I got home to find the front door was unlocked. I called the police right away. I didn't even go in until they came. The men were missing at the hospital this afternoon when I visited Peter. I told the police about them."

"That was smart. But you didn't tell them about Peter's office?" Did Teresa think she could protect Peter somehow?

"If there's something they're after in his work, I want to know it first." Teresa glanced at me as if pausing before a leap.

"Peter and I haven't been happy for a long time, but I owe him some loyalty." Her teeth curled over her full lip again. "Especially because I've become involved with someone else."

"Juan Carlos Vega?"

"How did you know?"

"I put some things together."

"You have a lot of intuition. I sensed that about you the day you came to my house."

Teresa turned left and drove two blocks to the parking lot at Bauman Hall. The department of Plant Biology wasn't far away.

We walked swiftly, not talking much, entering the building with Teresa's key, and taking the elevator to Peter's office on the second floor. Teresa opened the office with a second key and closed the door. Peter's office was not what I expected, not the office of a man who carried corn bread in his pockets. It was large and extremely neat. The lustrous mahogany desk facing the door was almost bare, except for a laptop, a lamp, a pad of paper, and a pen. A matching bookcase on the back wall held rows of books, all neatly shelved. A brown leather couch sat to the right of the door with a reading lamp, a small table, and a large, round stone that looked like a giant paperweight. So this was the couch Peter had used with Mei Lee. I couldn't help wondering if it pulled out to a bed. An office smelling faintly of books and furniture polish was hardly a romantic environment.

"Spartan," I said.

"Yes, Peter's office is a little island of order in a very messy life."

I tried the desk drawers. Two were locked. "Do you have the key to these drawers?"

"No, Peter wouldn't go that far."

"Where could he have put a key?" I scanned the office. There were no containers or boxes. I began to walk around the room, looking under the couch, lifting its cushions, raising the large stone paperweight, moving the lamp, and feeling along the top of the door. Where else did TV detectives look? I studied the bookcase. There was something a little off. Every book was lined up straight except for one on the lower right corner. I walked to the bookcase, stooped, and carefully pulled out the book. A small key fell to the floor.

"I'll bet this is it." I unlocked both the drawers, and Teresa kneeled down to examine their contents. The smaller one contained a set of computer disks. The bigger drawer held hanging files. Teresa slipped the set of CDs into the tiny purse she wore across her chest.

"Peter's lab notes," she said, "but let's see what he has in these files." She removed some files and settled into the couch, legs folded, hair cascading around her face, and began to read. I turned on the computer.

"Do you know his password?"

"No, that was secret too."

I stared at the screen. "Pigs," I typed. Then, one by one, "hogs," "swine," "boar," "sow," "porcine," "hog barn," "hog farm," "pigsty," "hog feed." This was getting nowhere.

"What was the name of Peter's new corn?" I asked Teresa.

"Double Dare."

I typed in "Double Dare." Zilch. But pigs and corn weren't Peter's only interests. I entered "Teresa." Nothing. Then "Jenny." Zip. "Mei Lee." No. Then, on a hunch, I typed in Mei Lee's nickname, "Beautiful Plum." The computer screen came alive. I turned to Peter's e-mails, and for fifteen minutes the two of us read silently.

"Oh, *Dios*," Teresa said.

"What'd you find?"

"Peter had a contract with Syndicon giving them first rights on patenting any of his discoveries. That was one of his corrupt practices. He'd done it before."

"I thought the university didn't permit that kind of thing."

"Peter did it anyway. Syndicon's about to launch a genetically engineered corn that's resistant to insects and disease. It was Peter's discovery, and it was going to make them both tons of money. But over the summer he seems to have found some data about the negative effects of this particular corn on pigs."

"Maybe that explains these e-mails to Syndicon. Take a look at this list I've sorted out." I stood up, and Teresa took my place.

"Yes, he's referring to his research in this one."

Teresa read through the e-mails, then looked up at me, her face drained of its usual color.

"Peter was threatening to go public with his results. Syndicon forbade him to do so on the grounds that it would reveal trade secrets. That's what they do to prevent researchers from blowing the whistle on things they don't want the public to know. Syndicon is famous for saying right out loud that their responsibility is to market products and that responsibility for establishing their safety rests with the FDA." Teresa gave her hair a twist and secured it in a low ponytail with a band she'd taken from her purse. "Of course the data they give the FDA often lacks critical information on the grounds that it's a trade secret too. It's the greediest, most corrupt operation you can imagine. And they're extremely aggressive in court, and out against anyone who threatens their profits or reputation."

I looked into Teresa's eyes, which had grown larger as she talked. They reminded me of Juan Carlos's.

"Was Peter going to blow the whistle on Syndicon?"

"Yes, I think he was blackmailing them to keep him silent."

"Or did he suddenly develop a conscience?"

Teresa frowned, then glanced at Peter's desk as if trying to read its meaning.

"Peter loved those pigs. He'd been around them all his life. Maybe he was taking up their cause by threatening to go public."

"Either way, Peter probably *was* being followed and harassed. That happens to people who threaten to reveal corporate corruptions. The two men at the hospital were probably involved. As long as Peter was in a coma, the information about the pigs was safe, but when he came out of it, he became a danger again. That robbery at your house this afternoon—they were after his data."

"But they didn't get it because Peter doesn't keep it on his home computer." Teresa returned to the couch and continued to read while I scrolled through e-mails.

Click. The door opened with a low sound, and two men in chinos, plaid shirts, and highly polished black shoes appeared. One held a briefcase. Oh, I thought, it's the men in black suits I saw at Halloween. They've disguised themselves as scientists, but they've gotten the shoes all wrong. Both were tall and clean-shaven, one thin, one blond and thick. The thin man was wearing rimless glasses. Both looked straight at me and the computer.

"We'll take that laptop," Rimless Glasses said.

"And we'll take the contents of those drawers," Blondie added. He had a large round face and looked as if he could have been jolly, only he wasn't.

"They don't belong to you," I said.

"On the contrary, I believe they do. It's in Professor Elliott's contract. We're only taking what is rightly ours."

"Please step away from the computer," the thin one said. His hand rose from his hip revealing a small, stainless steel gun.

I stood up slowly. Shouldn't they be wearing their suits? I had a hard time putting the gun together with the shirts and chinos.

Rimless leaned over to close the lid of the laptop. Blondie began to rummage through the drawers, turning his back to me. I looked at Teresa and then at the large stone paperweight on the edge of the table. The open door had hidden Teresa and the couch. I raised my leg in a quick left forward kick that sent the thin man sprawling on the desk. Pivoting, I caught Blondie with a right roundhouse to the side of his back using all my strength. He plunged forward onto the back of his companion.

Teresa picked up the paperweight and brought it down on the side of the thick man's head. The two of us bolted through the door, ran to the end of the hall and down the backstairs, and pushed through the door into the chilly air.

It was night now. We sprinted between the tall shadowy trees on Biology Way, swerved left at Engineering, then right along a road that ran beside the Hog Barn.

"Let's see if the Hog Barn is open," I said. "The door's on the other side." I suddenly longed for the warmth and innocence of the baby pigs. We skirted the pens where the giant hogs were no more than inky forms and a piercing odor. The white double doors on the front side of the barn were locked. I pounded on them and yelled for help, but no one answered. Inside I could hear the high squeals of piglets.

"We don't have time for this," Teresa said. "They won't be out long, and at least one of them had a gun."

"Okay, the parking lot." We skirted the far end of the Institute for Analytical Dynamics. One window was lit. I looked at it longingly, wishing it were Wilmer's, but even if it were, we could never make ourselves heard. The parking lot, which lay adjacent to the Institute, was empty except for three cars. Teresa's white Volvo, faintly illuminated by a single light, looked apparitional. We dashed across the lot, but as we got closer to the car we saw that all four tires had been slashed. How did they know this was our car? I wondered. But we had driven Teresa's sedan. The men who'd been following Peter must have known both family vehicles.

"Your office?" I asked breathlessly.

"They probably know where my office is."

"Then let's keep going. Maybe we'll see some lights and find a building that's open. Haven Hall. The computer lab. There'll be people there." For a change, the annoying computer lab seemed like a good idea. "We're on the other side of campus, but we're near the arboretum. It will lead us back, and we won't be so exposed."

We ran across the lot and found the road to the arboretum trail, hurried across, and turned left. The dusky trees of the arboretum swallowed us. It was a different world in darkness. We slowed our pace to catch our breath and walked quietly and quickly in the night. A Delta Breeze carried the low sound of voices. Someone was behind us in the distance. We had almost reached the prickly pear and giant yucca of the arboretum and saw the outline of the palm trees rise against the sky. But the path beyond the trees was lit. Lights in the arboretum? I'd never noticed them during the day.

"Wait," I said. "If we keep going, they're going to see us." I looked around. Beyond us to the north the giant legs of the water tower loomed pale and ghostly in the darkness, its usual lights extinguished. I remembered how I had studied the tower on my walk with Helena and then how I had climbed the tower in my dream, the campus lights spread out beneath me, and something about the tower began to compel me, to draw me in. "There's a ladder on the far leg of the water tower. If we climb it, we'll be off the ground and since we're wearing black, we'll be hard to see. We're a threat to them now that we've seen what they're up to."

"Are you crazy?" But then we heard the nearby sound of a car backfiring or perhaps a shot.

Teresa grabbed my hand. We edged our way through the bushes and ran into the darkened space around the water tower legs. Someone had parked a university vehicle next to the ladder, which was eight feet off the ground. Perhaps an employee had been working on the lights.

"If we get on the truck's roof," I said quietly, "we can reach the ladder." I forced myself not to look up at the towering structure. Focus, I thought. It's like the kickboxing bag. Just look at what's in front of you. I climbed onto the hood and then the truck's roof and reached for the ladder. I knew the climb was straight up, one hand over the other, one foot after the next. I looked at my hands in front of me and began to climb. I felt Teresa just behind.

"*Madre!*" Teresa said softly. "Mother of God."

We ascended without a word until my legs began to ache, my arms to burn. I paused.

"Let's rest." I could hear Teresa breathing right below me. Suddenly, a flap of wings and a feathery thing flew past me, and a surge of weakness pulsed through my hands and arms and legs. I began to feel the familiar dizziness I'd always experienced with heights. My hands began to slip, and I saw my body on the ground and Polly, motherless. But then as if a dam had broken and emptied its watery force into a dried streambed, a flow of energy filled me, and I closed my hands more tightly on the rung.

"A bird," I said at last. "Maybe a dove. It must have been nesting somewhere. Okay," I said and reached for the next rung. I thought of the push-ups I'd done in class. "Twenty push-ups," my instructor had yelled. "Now twenty more. You can do it!" The metal rods bruised my palms and bit through my thin leather shoes into the bottoms of my feet. But we were near the top and I had not looked down, not even once. We climbed the final rungs. I counted them to myself the way I'd counted the seconds when I'd squatted, my thighs on fire, against the wall in class.

At the top of the ladder, I scrambled under the metal railing that ran along a narrow ledge. We'd reached the catwalk that encircled the dome. Tightly grasping the railing, I edged sideways to make room for Teresa, and in a moment I felt the weight of her body hit the ledge and smelled the faint plum and rose of her perfume. We stood side by side, breathing deeply, fifteen stories above the ground.

The campus lay beneath us, a patterned mass of dark with twinkling lights. It's beautiful, I reflected, if I could just stop thinking about where I was. Never in my life would I have imagined myself at the top of this tower. How had I dared? Had the dream prepared me in some way? And if I ever got down from here, would I dream about the tower again, would I have overcome my fear of heights? Sweat curled down my chest, but the metal bar was cold and soon I felt the chill. I looked down and saw a light in the pool of dark below.

"They must have known we wouldn't follow a lighted path," I said softly. "They're taking a look around." The light bounced off the truck beneath us, and I could hear the growl of voices.

"Can you tell what they're saying?" I whispered to Teresa.

"No."

"Can you stand to look down the ladder?"

"I'm looking. Oh, *Dios*! They're coming up!"

For a brief moment, I imagined myself and Teresa being pushed from the catwalk to the distant ground below, two figures dressed in black sailing forward into a moonless night, but this time I had the presence of mind to steady myself by hooking my hands on the metal bar.

"Maybe we can dislodge them," I said, remembering the dove and how the suddenness of its feathery flight had almost made me lose my grip. "Let's throw our shoes," I said. I was wearing flats. I took them off and Teresa removed her heavy clogs. Then one after another we hurled them quickly down the ladder.

"What the hell?" we heard. Then a cry and another cry.

Teresa peered over the edge. "I think the first guy fell on the other and knocked him off."

I looked carefully over the railing, both hands gripping the metal rail. It was impossible to see anything on the ground. The night was still, and we stood rigidly, like ancient statues in the gloom, until headlights cut through the tomb-like dark and a red light flashed. It was a campus police car, and we could hear the fluty sound of women's voices.

"Help," I yelled down.

"We're up here at the top. We were being chased."

"Wait there," I heard a woman's voice call back. "Don't try to climb. We'll have the fire department get you down."

Teresa looked down the ladder. The headlights of the car had illuminated the scene underneath. "They're loading the two men into the back of the police car."

I felt the tension draining from my body, but my mouth still tasted of metal. After what seemed like hours, a fire truck arrived, lights flashing. And Teresa and I climbed down to the cherry picker that received us and lowered us gently to the truck and then down to the welcome earth. Two officers walked up to us.

"Professor Addams?" It was Sergeants Gina Garcia and Dorothy Brown.

"I'm so glad to see you. This is Professor Teresa Fuentes-Elliott."

"Hi, Officers. I know them both," Teresa said. "They've been to see me plenty."

Gina slowly shook her head, as if to say, what next? She'd seen me and Teresa too, evidently, way too much.

Another police car arrived. We searched for and found our shoes.

"We'll take you to the police station first," Dorothy said quietly, "and then we'll get you home."

★ ★ ★

Teresa and I shivered at a metal table in the station as we told the story of our day and evening.

"We've had our eyes on these two for a while, ever since they started hanging out at the hospital like turkey vultures," Gina said. "I'd guess they were waiting to see if Professor Elliott would come out of his coma."

"That would have solved Syndicon's problem all right," I said. "What lengths would they have gone to if Peter hadn't been in a coma in the first place?" Had Lorna's corn bread, unbeknownst to her, momentarily placed her unfaithful lover out of greater harm's way? Peter had easily manipulated Lorna, but in challenging Syndicon's control he'd reached too far. He was lucky to have ended up in the muck beside the pig's pen. At least he was alive.

"We'll drive you home," Dorothy said.

I remembered my purse.

"Could you take us to Peter's office first? I left my purse there."

Dorothy let us in using her master keys. Peter's office bore only the slightest trace of the scuffle. His laptop was on the floor with his pen and paperweight. Teresa picked up the laptop.

"I think we'll need that," Dorothy said gently.

"You'll need these too," Teresa said sheepishly as she handed over the CDs in her purse.

My turquoise leather purse lay near the desk, seemingly untouched. I hung it on my shoulder. It sagged heavily. I was glad I hadn't had it on the run. Gina drove us both to Wild Deer Lane.

"We'll talk," I said. Teresa and I embraced, and then I drove home.

The grinning pumpkin on the front porch stared at me darkly. I'd forgotten it was Halloween. Fortunately, no tricks had been played on me at home. On campus it had been a different story. Malevolent forces had unleashed themselves and run amok. It was twelve o'clock, and I was soon in bed. At 3:00 a.m. my phone rang once and stopped. The phone company was keeping its promise. Perhaps it was a student after all—I'd surmised from Alma and the police that such pranks were not uncommon. At least Hallows' Eve had passed, and it was now El Dia de Los Muertos.

Tess's Genetically Engineered Corn Bread

2 tablespoons butter
2 eggs
¼ cup GE canola or corn oil
2 tablespoons honey
1 cup buttermilk
1 cup GE cornmeal (freshly ground if possible)
½ cup whole wheat flour (freshly ground if possible)
½ cup barley flour (freshly ground if possible)
½ teaspoon salt
2 teaspoons baking powder

Preheat oven to 425°F.

Place 2 tablespoons of butter into an 8-inch square pan. Set pan in oven while it is heating.

Beat eggs. Then add oil, honey, and buttermilk to them.

Add dry ingredients, gently mixing.

Pour batter into the preheated pan and bake for 25 minutes.

Adapted by permission of Pam Ronald from *Tomorrow's Table: Organic Farming, Genetics, and the Future of Food* by Pamela C. Ronald and Raoul W. Adamchak. (Oxford University Press, 2008.)

Epilogue

I lay in bed. It was cold and too early for the heater to kick in. My thighs and arms ached, my palms and the soles of my feet felt raw, and the top of my right foot bore a dark purple bruise. Kicking a padded bag was a different thing from landing a blow on a human body. I'd often wondered whether kickboxing could be a form of self-defense, and now that I'd proved it could, I felt amazed and stunned that I'd pulled it off. The kicks had probably saved our skins, the kicks and our crazed ascent of the water tower. Not experiences I was eager to repeat any time ever, but this morning, my state of shock still unabated, they seemed far off, like frightening sequences in a really bad dream.

What will come of this? I wondered. What will happen to Peter Elliott? Will he be physically impaired? Disciplined by the university? Lose his job? Or will he slip right back into the privileged place that was his usual habitat? Will others like Collin Morehead take Peter's place? Collin hadn't poisoned Peter, but there was plenty of the noxious in him. With the arrest of the Syndicon representatives—were they representatives or hit men, maybe both?—Peter's double dipping and his data about Double Dare Corn would be revealed. Maybe, there would be greater scrutiny of corporate ties, greater reflection on the role of greed and corporate profit in university research. Perhaps Arbor State's historically communal spirit would reassert itself against the culture of me-first, profit-driven values that had become so familiar in the last few years. The university's long-standing collegiality, after all, had formed part of the environment in which our own smaller union of women's, ethnic, and American studies had come about.

I thought of Lorna once again, of the weariness on her face when it had dawned upon her that a long, hard migration lay ahead. Since Peter hadn't died, Lorna wouldn't be tried for murder, but there was a law against knowingly poisoning food, whether you served it up or not. I thought it a good law. Trust in food was a basic social need, a foundation that helped communities form and sustain themselves and make life feel good. Lorna would be subject to that law, and, in contrast to Peter's, Lorna's future looked bleak. It didn't seem fair. In many ways, after all, Peter had poisoned himself. He'd helped himself to the corn bread that Lorna had decided not to feed to him, and he'd partaken of Syndicon's pernicious values so completely and for so long that his whole being had been turned toxic. Alma had said that those who live by dog-eat-dog rules often turn on each other—like pigs biting each other's tails. Peter had shown that they could, unwittingly, do themselves in as well.

The room had warmed and so had I. I would start my day slowly—a long shower, hot coffee, the paper, two poached eggs on toast. The sky dazzled me with blue when I picked up my paper outside, and the air carried the good, earthy smell of fallen leaves. A good day for going on. I would make the corn pudding later, just before I went onto campus, so it would stay warm for the celebration. I would make it in a calm state of mind, and I would taste it carefully. It had a sweetness to it because of the corn and because of the six tablespoons of sugar that made it almost seem like a dessert, but it was not dessert. It was a staple. For many it was the basis of life itself.

I thought about how food, and even ideas about food,

connected people. For some Native Americans, growth, life, the feminine were associated with Corn Mother. Navajos believed that men and women were born from ears of corn. For Mayans, too, humanity emerged from maize. Corn was "our mother," "our life," "she who sustains us." Isokana, an African deity of agriculture, was responsible for making corn grow. The Japanese Inari Okami was the god or goddess of rice and of fertility. The Greek goddess Demeter, who was associated with grain, was also a symbol of abundance and plenty. Demeter had descended to the underworld and risen up, bringing restoration and rebirth. It was no surprise that food and rebirth were so often deified. I thought about my frightening encounter with the two men in Peter's office, about my flight with Teresa, our struggle to ascend the water tower, and about this day of coming back into my ordinary existence. The celebration of El Dia de Los Muertos would be an occasion for my own renewal.

Later that afternoon, I made the corn pudding. There was a simplicity to creating the dish that I enjoyed. I cracked four eggs into the food processor, measured the milk and cream and dumped them in. Then sugar, a bit of flour, a little baking powder, melted butter, and half the defrosted corn. I whizzed it all until it was pureed and then added the rest of the corn and buzzed the processor just to mix. The whole kernels would give the pudding texture. I wasn't grinding corn as millions of women before me had done—thank God for the food processor. But this labor of planning the dish, gathering the ingredients, mixing the batter, baking—all the while anticipating the pleasure of those I would feed—linked me to women throughout the ages. And also to men, but it was mainly women who had cooked day to day, who had sustained life, solidified family and community ties, marked unifying ritual occasions with special foods, and seen to it that life maintained this form of nurturing, pleasure, and creating solidarity.

Now, what to wear to the celebration? The more color, the

better. My colleagues would be wearing their brightest clothes today too. A long wine-colored skirt—I preferred long skirts—a wine-colored long-sleeved T-shirt, a black jacket, and, of course, turquoise earrings. Turquoise stood for strength, protection from harm, psychic sensitivity, and connection to the world of spirits. It brought good luck to the home as well. At the last moment I draped a turquoise scarf around my neck. Dressing up was another way of honoring one's community and of giving pleasure too. When the pudding was done, I wrapped it in foil to keep it warm, placed it on a jelly roll pan to keep it from sliding around in the back of my car, and carried it out the door. I needed to be with my community today, to feel its healing energies. I had a special pass and could park near Haven Hall. I'd made a double batch of corn pudding, and the dish was warm and heavy in my hands.

★ ★ ★

Upon entering the Chicana/o Studies seminar room, I went directly to the table reserved for food to be shared. The surface was already filling with plump, pale tamales wrapped in corn husks, dark chocolate mole, and a salad of black beans, red pepper, corn, and cilantro. Someone had baked a fragrant berry pie with deep purple juice seeping through the crust. I set the golden dish of pudding near the salad because the colors looked so good together. The room had been recently painted, and the resident Chicano artist had mixed the hue of paint himself—a deep Mexican blue. Everyone looked smashing against those walls. I wanted the formula. I wanted my bedroom to look like this. Even my pale coloring must look good against this vibrant blue. I thought of the second time that Wilmer and I had met, how he'd lingered at my eyes.

The students, staff, and faculty were creating an altar at one end of the room. Alma was arranging brilliant orange marigolds in a large rectangle on a red cloth background. The marigold's strong odor was meant to lead spirits to the altar. Isobel was lighting red votive candles. Their flickering light welcomed the spirits back. Antonio placed medium-sized sugar skulls inside the marigolds. They were elaborately decorated with icing and bits of foil in purples, pinks, greens, and oranges. Frank Walker came next with small plates of salt, representing the continuance of life. Yvonne added pan de muertos, rounds of bread with crossed bones on them, and a student brought water, lest the spirits be thirsty. Sticks of spicy incense already burned to beckon the dead, and in the very center of the table, red-draped steps held photographs of departed relatives and friends.

I saw a tattered picture of a young couple dressed for work in the fields. Were they Alma's parents? I placed a small photo of Miriam's delicate face alongside it. The bright colors of the room and of its tables would have pleased her. For a moment, I felt Miriam's spirit. She'd embodied so many of the things that had come to be important in my life, the sharing of food, the love of color, deep friendships with women and men, a hunger for community and a larger purpose, and an appreciation of the joy they all gave to life.

Isobel, wearing a turquoise shirt and a dark violet skirt— it struck me that my love of color had come from Isobel as well—set a picture of a young man with a long, dark ponytail on the altar. Her nephew, I thought. I went up to her and we embraced. Early November was a sad time for both of us.

"We held a cleansing last night in Haven Hall," Isobel said quietly.

"A cleansing?" Isobel looked at me as if she were sharing a secret I was a little slow to guess.

"You know, fire, incense, bird feathers."

"Ah." I understood that peyote had been involved and that the feathers would have come from a large, predatory bird like an eagle, a bird with the power to protect. My Native American colleagues had come together to purify and protect the community of Haven Hall and would have stayed quite late. I thought about the dove's appearance on the water tower, about the sudden surge of energy that had allowed me to hang on despite the weakness in my arms. Were the cleansing and that unlooked-for power connected?

The sound of voices rose like a swell of music, reminding me of a party at my house the previous winter when Isobel had brought CDs of cumbia and everyone had danced. Now that memory blended with other memories of Frank's meditation on community, of the meeting with a view of the treetops at which we had first considered a formal unification, of Isobel standing next to the fire's illuminating warmth. Those moments merged with this one as the room filled with colleagues, many from outside our six programs. Frank Walker stood in a knot of students, listening and smiling. I walked over to him and touched his arm.

"Emily, I'm glad you've come." He was wearing a bolo tie and corduroy jacket, his ponytail tied with a leather cord.

I thought about his talk that night in Bauman Hall. Our community today was an embodiment of what he'd said that evening about the connection of all to all. I saw Ursula across the room wearing gigantic red earrings and then caught a glimpse of Helena's pale yellow hair. I thought of how relieved Helena would be to hear that, for a time at least, the vandals and their threats had been put to rest. Helena was talking to Callie and Grace. Grace had been right about Mei Lee's innocence. Mei Lee would graduate in peace. I made my way to the circle they formed, knowing I'd never felt as close to my colleagues as I did that day, knowing I'd never been so happy just standing firmly on a floor. For one moment I remembered how my arms and hands had gone weak on the ladder when the dove flapped past me, how I might have fallen, taking Teresa with me. But I had not.

"Emily," Helena said, making room for me, but Alma was about to make a speech.

"We come together today," Alma said, dressed for the occasion in a traditional white Mexican blouse with flowers and vines in red, blue, and yellow, "to remember those who have left us, but even more to celebrate the joy they brought to our lives, to know that we too live in the face of mortality. Let this knowledge make us mindful of how we treat each other, of the blessings of this world, of our communities, and of the community we make together."

El Dia de Los Muertos took such a positive approach to death and to the world of spirits. It welcomed the spirits, celebrated them, affirmed mortality, and made something positive and grimly humorous of it all. It reminded people that the dead remained with them. What Miriam had stood for lived on in me, just as Isobel's nephew lived on in her and Alma's parents in her as well. The table held sugar skeletons dressed in traditional Mexican costumes. A bride and her groom, a dancer in a flaring dress of red, white, and green, her partner in black and silver. Polly would have liked those skeletons. I would ask if I could take one back to her. I thought of Wilmer, of how I wished he could share this moment too. I'd invited him, but he hadn't committed, had talked of his need to work, and said he'd think about coming near the end. I wondered if he'd bother to show up.

"I have an announcement to make," Antonio said as Alma ended. "I heard from the administration today that our petition has been granted, at least in part. We're to become a separate, named unit in the Division of Humanities. Vice Provost Vogle had opposed this, as some of you know, but late last week, she changed her mind."

Well, I thought, a good way for Lorna to go out. I wondered if our encounter in her office had brought about this change. Lorna, however momentarily, seemed to have reverted to the woman who cared about collectivity, the woman who'd studied migratory birds. Now she'd made it possible for our community to continue on firmer ground. I looked at Callie in her gold hoop earrings. She was one of the younger generation who would inherit the outcome of our collective work.

"Let's have a toast," Antonio said. "There's wine and juice here and atole, which, if you haven't had it, is made of masa and cinnamon and sugar. Here's to our new life together, the beginning of a new era."

Glasses were raised and liquids drunk. Isobel approached and took my hand.

"We've done it," Isobel said.

It was a rare moment of feeling fully joyful and triumphant. I thought of how pleased Isobel would be when she heard of Lorna's confession. Now, Frank would no longer be a suspect, and Yvonne's employment would be safe. The people she'd been so determined to protect had escaped significant harm. From a distance, I could see Alma's face, lit like one of the candles. The idea of formally uniting had come from her. We had arrived at this place together, each doing a part, and, for a moment, though I knew such times were fleeting, our connection to each other felt utopian.

"Have you heard," Helena asked, "that Lorna Vogle has gone on extended leave? Her office was apparently cleaned out over Halloween weekend."

After the celebration was over, I would have to tell Lorna's story to Isobel, Alma, Helena, Grace, Ursula, Callie, and Wilmer too. I would have to tell the story of the two men and the gun and the climb on the water tower. Peter Elliott would have to face the music and so would Lorna. Teresa and Juan Carlos would need to figure out their lives. I imagined they would figure out their lives together. But that was for another day. This moment was for healing, for reaffirming our ties to each other and our ties elsewhere, a time of recalling the many kinds of communities that are possible, for celebrating the idea of community itself—as a bulwark against loss, mortality, and despair. It was a time for resting and breaking bread and for filling up the reservoir of trust. We would need that reservoir, I was certain, in the times to come. I clinked my glass against Isobel's. Neither of us knew what the new millennium would bring, and at that moment, Wilmer Crane, tall, bespectacled, and smiling, appeared at the door. Perhaps he, too, would be part of my future.

Blue Corn Atole

1 cup milk
2 teaspoons piloncillo
(Mexican sugar cones) or
¼ cup brown sugar with
2 tablespoons molasses
4 teaspoons roasted blue
cornmeal★

1 stick cinnamon (canela)
or ¼ teaspoon ground
cinnamon
1 vanilla bean split length-
wise or 2 teaspoons
vanilla extract

Add milk and cornmeal together and stir until combined (can be heated on stove or with cappuccino or espresso steamer).

Heat it just until it begins to thicken.

Add vanilla seeds (scraped from inside the bean) or vanilla flavoring, piloncillo or brown sugar, and cinnamon stick or ground cinnamon. Serve hot in mugs.

Adapted from The Cooking Post: Traditional Native American Recipes at http://www.cookingpost.com/recipes.htm.

★Roasted blue cornmeal available from The Cooking Post at http://www.cookingpost.com/viewItem.asp?idProduct=27

More Food for Thought

Blue Corn Bread

1 cup Tamaya brand blue cornmeal★
1 cup all-purpose flour
2 tablespoons sugar
1 tablespoons baking powder
½ teaspoon salt
2 large eggs
1 cup milk
¼ cup butter or margarine

Preheat oven to 400°F.

Combine dry ingredients.

Beat eggs with milk and blend in butter or margarine.

Stir liquids into dry mixture—just to moisten.

Spoon into muffin cups (2½-inch size).

Bake on center rack in the preheated oven for 30 to 35 minutes, until the edges of the corn bread pull away from the sides of the dish and a toothpick inserted into the center comes out clean. Let cool 10 minutes before cutting.

Adapted from The Cooking Post: Traditional Native American Recipes at http://www.cookingpost.com/recipes.htm.

★Cornmeal available from The Cooking Post at http://www.cooking-post.com/viewItem.asp?idProduct=28

Savory Corn Bread Muffins with Jalapeños and Corn

1 cup yellow cornmeal,
  preferably organic
  stone-ground
1 cup whole-wheat flour
¾ teaspoon salt
2 teaspoons baking
  powder
1 teaspoon baking soda
1 tablespoon finely
  chopped fresh sage or 1

teaspoon rubbed sage
2 eggs
1½ cups buttermilk
¼ cup canola oil
1 tablespoon honey
1 cup corn kernels
2 tablespoons minced
  jalapeños
½ cup grated Cheddar or
  Monterey Jack (optional)

Place rack in the upper third of the oven and preheat the oven to 400°F.

Oil or butter muffin tins.

Put cornmeal into a bowl, and then sift the flour, salt, baking powder, and baking soda into it. Add sage and stir.

Beat eggs with buttermilk, oil, and honey in another bowl.

Stir, but do not beat, the dry corn bread ingredients into the liquid ingredients. The resulting mixture can have some lumps, but do not leave flour in the bottom of the bowl.

Add corn kernels, jalapeño, and cheese.

Spoon the mixture into muffin cups about 4/5 full.

Bake 20 to 25 minutes. They should be lightly browned and well risen.

These will last for a couple of days in or out of the refrigerator and for several in the freezer.

Adapted by permission of Martha Rose
Shulman from http://cooking.nytimes.com/
recipes/1013497-savory-cornbread-muffins-with-jalapenos-and-corn.

Corn Pudding

4 cups frozen corn kernels (about 19 ounces), thawed
4 large eggs
1 cup whipping cream
½ cup whole milk
6 tablespoons sugar
¼ cup (½ stick) butter, room temperature
2 tablespoons all-purpose flour
2 teaspoons baking powder
1 teaspoon salt

Preheat oven to 350°F and butter an 8 x 8 x 2-inch baking dish.

Using half of the corn, blend all ingredients in processor until almost smooth.

Add remaining corn to the processor and process briefly to mix.

Pour batter into the buttered dish. Bake pudding for about 45 minutes or until the top is brown and the center is just set. Cool ten minutes and serve.

Adapted from *Epicurious* http://www.epicurious.com/recipes/food/
views/sweet-corn-pudding-102683.

Aterword

Although *Oink: A Food for Thought Mystery* is a work of fiction, some elements of it are based on my own experience. In the 1990s, the state was imposing budget cuts on my university, and the continued funding of the women's, American, and four ethnic studies programs was frequently in doubt. In response to the threat of being defunded or merged into large departments, the six programs formed a unified community in which reflection, struggle, friendship, food, and pleasure were key to the organizing process. Women in science on campus were also suffering many inequities in hiring, promotion, and access to resources, and a group of women were writing grant proposals for money with which to address those issues.

By 2016, five of the six small programs had become departments—with greater security than programs—and the sixth was in the process of becoming one too. The women who organized to improve the situation of women in science on campus had received two grants for promoting the advancement of women and underrepresented minorities in science, technology, engineering, and mathematics (or STEM), with an emphasis on understanding some of the challenges faced by Latina faculty in particular.

The lesson I take from this is that forming and organizing as collegial communities on campus can accomplish a great deal and that communities which involve the often-invisible labor of "working on the relationship" are especially powerful. This labor includes getting folks together, listening to people's needs, building face-to-face relationships of friendship, love, and trust, deflecting conflict, mending fences, hosting dinners, engaging in playfulness and pleasure, and, in general, tending to people's hunger for connection and community.

In academic and other work cultures, where we are frequently beset by isolation, competition, lack of solidarity, and overwork, our happiness and quality of life, not to mention our struggles for social justice, may depend not just on forming communities but on persisting in the sometimes hard, but often joyful, labor of making them work.

Recipe Index

Credits

Recipe for Corn and Cherry Scones adapted by permission of the Cheese Board Collective at http://cheeseboardcollective. coop/. From *The Cheese Board Collective Works* (Berkeley: Ten Speed Press, 2003.)

Recipe for Oven Polenta, Tomato Fondue, and Sonoma Jack Cheese adapted by permission of Gary Danko, Chef, Restaurant Gary Danko. From *Lee Bailey's California Wine Country Cooking* (New York: Clarkson Potter/Publishers, 1991).

Recipe for Southern Corn Bread with kind permission of Mattie Smith Nettles.

Recipe for Red Enchiladas adapted by permission of Mely Martinez at Mexico in My Kitchen http://www. mexicoinmykitchen.com/2013/05/red-enchiladas-sauce-recipereceta.html.

Recipe for Baked Tortilla Chips by permission of www. Allrecipes.com. Recipe submitted by Michele O'Sullivan.

Recipe for Corn with Pine Nuts adapted by permission of Annie Taylor Chen at VeganAnn http://veganann.com/corn-with-pine-nuts/.

Recipe for Wild Georgia Shrimp and Grits adapted by permission of Ron Eyester.

Recipe for Corn Muffins adapted by permission of Mel at Mel's Kitchen Cafe at http://www.melskitchencafe.com/cornbread-muffins/.

Recipe for Gluten-Free Cornmeal Pancakes with Candied Kumquats adapted by permission of Rachel Leung and Rachel Chew at http://www.radiantrachels.com/gluten-free-cornmeal-pancakes-with-candied-kumquats/#comment.

Recipe for Blue Corn Blini with Smoked Salmon adapted by permission of Taralee Lathrop at My Kitchen Ink http://www.mykitchenink.com/recipes/auth_1/recipe/75/.

Recipe for Colombian Corn and Cheese Arepas adapted by permission of Julia Moskin. From http://cooking.nytimes.com/recipes/1015180-colombian-corn-and-cheese-arepas.

Recipe for Candy Corn Halloween Cupcakes adapted by permission of Holly and Katie at The SemiSweet Sisters http://www.thesemisweetsisters.com/2014/09/19/candy-corn-halloween-cupcakes/.

Recipe for Corn Bread with Caramelized Onions and Goat Cheese adapted by permission of Deb Perelman at Smitten Kitchen http://smittenkitchen.com/blog/2009/03/caramelized-onion-and-goat-cheese-cornbread/. Corn Bread with Caramelized Onions and Goat Cheese was originally published on SmittenKitchen.com. All content and photos © 2006–2016 Smitten Kitchen LLC.

Recipe for Tess's Genetically Engineered Corn Bread adapted by permission of Pam Ronald, professor in the Genome Center and the Department of Plant Pathology, founding faculty director of the Institute for Food and Agricultural Literacy (IFAL) at UC Davis, and director of Grass Genetics at the Joint BioEnergy Institute in Emeryville, California. From *Tomorrow's Table: Organic Farming, Genetics, and the Future of Food* by Pamela C. Ronald and Raoul W. Adamchak. (Oxford University Press, 2008.)

Recipe for Blue Corn Atole adapted from The Cooking Post: Traditional Native American Recipes at http://www.cookingpost.com/recipes.htm.

Recipe for Blue Corn Bread adapted from The Cooking Post: Traditional Native American Recipes at http://www.cookingpost.com/recipes.htm.

Recipe for Savory Corn Bread Muffins with Jalapeños and Corn adapted by permission of Martha Rose Shulman. From http://cooking.nytimes.com/recipes/1013497-savory-cornbread-muffins-with-jalapenos-and-corn.

Recipe for Corn Pudding adapted from *Epicurious* at http://www.epicurious.com/recipes/food/views/sweet-corn-pudding-102683.

Acknowledgments

Writing is at once lonely and communal, and the more communal it is, the better it feels. Many people have read pieces and/or early drafts of this work, and while they're not responsible for the final outcome, they helped me shape *Oink*, my first piece of fiction. I want to thank the following for being part of the village that guided and supported me: Elizabeth Kracht, Brooke Warner (my wonderful publisher), Mardi Louisell, Kay Trimberger, Tina Gillis, Wendy Martin, Claire Kahane, Susan Kaiser, Anna Kuhn, Pam Ronald, Diane Fowlkes, Linda Joy Myers, and anonymous press reviewers. A special thanks to my husband, Bill Tilden, for always being my first reader and critic and for his patience and loving support. I am also grateful to the editors and authors involved with She Writes Press and for the savvy and supportive community they and we have created.

About the Author

J. L. Newton is Professor Emerita at a land grant university. She is at work on another mystery and lives in California where she tends her garden and cooks for family and friends. You can contact her at jnjocals@gmail.com, www.facebook.com/ TastingHomeComingOfAgeInTheKitchen, at judithnewton. com, and on Twitter: @jnewton70.

SELECTED TITLES FROM SHE WRITES PRESS

She Writes Press is an independent publishing company
founded to serve women writers everywhere.
Visit us at www.shewritespress.com.

A Girl Like You: A Henrietta and Inspector Howard Novel by Michelle Cox
$16.95, 978-1-63152-016-7
When the floor matron at the dance hall where Henrietta works as a taxi
dancer turns up dead, aloof Inspector Clive Howard appears on the scene—
and convinces Henrietta to go undercover for him, plunging her into
Chicago's gritty underworld.

The Great Bravura by Jill Dearman
$16.95, 978-1-63152-989-4
Who killed Susie—or did she actually disappear? The Great Bravura, a dash-
ing lesbian magician living in a fantastical and noirish 1947 New York City,
must solve this mystery—before she goes to the electric chair.

Just the Facts by Ellen Sherman
$16.95, 978-1-63152-993-1
The seventies come alive in this poignant and humorous story of a fearful
rookie reporter at a small-town newspaper who uncovers a big-time scandal.

Water On the Moon by Jean P. Moore
$16.95, 978-1-938314-61-2
When her home is destroyed in a freak accident, Lidia Raven, a divorced
mother of two, is plunged into a mystery that involves her entire family.

Murder Under The Bridge: A Palestine Mystery by Kate Raphael
$16.95, 978-1-63152-960-3
Rania, a Palestinian police detective with a young son, meets cheeky Jewish-
American feminist Chloe at an Israeli checkpoint—and soon becomes
embroiled in a murder case that implicates the highest echelons of the Israeli
military.

The Black Velvet Coat by Jill G. Hall
$16.95, 978-1-63152-009-9
When the current owner of a black velvet coat—a San Francisco artist in
search of inspiration—and the original owner, a 1960s heiress who fled her
affluent life fifty years earlier, cross paths, their lives are forever changed . . .
for the better.